GUILT'S SHADOW

Arturo Maquino

Published by

Arturo Maquino

Deckademy Pty Ltd

maquinoarturo@gmail.com

v.2.0.08

Contents

Dedicated to my beautiful wife and my two daughters; you all mean everything to me and you make me want to take on the entire world for you.

<u>CHAPTER 1</u> COURTROOM 11

THE JURY LEANED forward as one when Ms Ramirez delivered the blow that would awaken the trial—confirming she'd heard the argument that supposedly sparked a murder—unaware that Avery was already measuring the fifty metres of shadows that turned her certainty into a guess.

The judge fought to maintain command, his voice cutting through the rising tension from the witness stand. In the public gallery of Courtroom 11, Supreme Court of New South Wales, reporters' fingers moved steadily across laptops and notepads. No cameras or recordings were allowed inside, but the atmosphere carried its own weight: a charged hush broken only by the occasional cough, the rustle of paper, the soft creak of wooden benches as people shifted.

Justice Harlan Bluegum raised a single hand, palm forward. The associate seated to his right spoke clearly: "Silence in the court." The murmurs faded to near-quiet, leaving only the low hum of the air-conditioning and the distant traffic on King Street far below.

On the witness stand, the middle-aged woman in the navy blazer had just finished her evidence-in-chief for the Crown. She had testified that she saw the accused, Kristof Stanis, in a heated argument with his wife Elle outside their Marrickville home the night before the murder. Under cross-examination by defence counsel, however, the account had begun to fray: fifty metres away, poor street lighting, no glasses (though she normally wore them for distance), and her decision to come forward only after seeing the Crime Stoppers reward poster weeks later.

Crown Prosecutor Elias Turner sat at his table, arms folded, face impassive. A veteran of more than fifteen years prosecuting serious crime in Sydney, he knew better than to show frustration. The identification evidence had landed, however imperfectly; he could see it in the way several jurors were now sitting a little straighter, glancing toward the dock.

Avery Santos rose from the defence table with unhurried grace. He adjusted the single button on his charcoal suit—bespoke, dark enough to disappear in a crowd, sharp enough to command attention when he wanted it. At thirty-six, Avery had spent his entire career as a criminal defence solicitor-advocate in Sydney. Ten years of winning acquittals and hung juries in cases most barristers would have settled or lost. He was not the loudest voice in the legal precinct around Phillip Street, nor the one most often quoted in the Sydney Morning Herald. But among prosecutors, judges, and the tight circle of criminal lawyers who actually tried cases, his name carried weight. The best defence lawyer in the city, some said quietly. Others—those who had lost to him—called him ruthless with ethics, a man who found every crack in the Crown case and drove a wedge through it.

He did not raise his voice now. In this courtroom, volume was a sign of desperation.

"Your Honour," Avery said evenly, "I submit that the witness's identification evidence is so unreliable it should carry minimal weight. The concessions she has already made go directly to the reliability of her observation."

Justice Bluegum looked at him over half-moon reading glasses. A former Crown prosecutor who had taken silk before ascending to the bench, Bluegum presided with the calm certainty of a man who had rarely seen the Prosecution lose in matters like this. His acquittal rate in homicide trials was among the lowest in the Supreme Court. "Mr Santos, the evidence is before the jury. They will assess its probative value in due course. If you have further questions for the witness, proceed."

Avery gave a small nod of acknowledgment—no argument, no theatrics—and turned to the witness box.

"Ms Ramirez, you observed this alleged argument at approximately 10:47 pm From roughly how far away?"

"Fifty metres or so."

"And the streetlight closest to the Stanis residence—was it illuminated?"

"I… I'm not entirely sure. It was dark."

Avery paused just long enough for the answer to settle. "The photographs tendered as exhibits show that particular streetlight had been reported faulty for three weeks prior to the date in question, with no repair record. So you were looking at a figure in near darkness, from fifty metres. Would you agree there is a real possibility of mistaken identity under those circumstances?"

The witness shifted in her seat. "I recognised the jacket."

"A high-visibility construction jacket? The same type issued to site workers across the city—thousands of them?"

Turner rose. "Your Honour, I object. The question is argumentative."

"Objection allowed," Bluegum said promptly. "Mr Santos, rephrase."

Avery accepted the ruling without flicker. "Ms Ramirez, given the distance, the lighting conditions, and the commonality of such jackets, is it fair to say it is possible you saw someone other than Mr Stanis that night?"

A long pause. Then, quietly: "I suppose… yes. It's possible."

Avery let the concession sit. He returned to his seat beside Kristof Stanis.

Kristof sat rigid in the dock, hands clasped on the wooden rail, knuckles pale. Forty-two years old, broad-shouldered from years on building sites, he had the easy manner of a man who got along with everyone— foreman on a major inner-city residential project, quick with a joke over smoko, father to a six-year-old daughter and nine-year-old son. The kind of bloke who bought rounds after knock-off and never let a mate walk home alone. Now he looked smaller, diminished by the glass partition and the weight of twenty-seven stab wounds the Crown said he had inflicted on his wife in their own garage.

Avery leaned in slightly. "She cracked on the identification," he murmured. "The jury heard it. That's important."

Kristof gave a tight nod. "Still feels like I'm drowning."

"You're not," Avery said. "Not yet."

Avery thought about the value of all this testimony. An argument overheard by a neighbour, the night before the murder, even if it was between Kristof and Elle – what direct evidence would that have to the death of Elle the following night? He knew that's how he saw it, but also learned to not assume jurors are that smart or that capable. He knew that if it made the story fit in their minds, they would make it more important than it was. That's why he knew he had to attack every piece and each front.

Across the bar table, Turner gathered his notes with deliberate care. He glanced toward the defence table and offered the smallest nod—professional courtesy between opponents who had faced each other before. Turner believed Kristof Stanis was guilty; the forensics, the timeline, the lack of any credible alternative explanation. He prosecuted accordingly.

In the back row of the public gallery, Detective Jacob Barker sat with arms folded, jaw set. At forty-three, Barker was still the handsome cop who turned heads—dark hair greying at the temples, steady gaze. He had led the investigation from day one: crime scene attendance, witness canvass, interviews, the lot. He despised defence lawyers on principle; they existed, in his view, to twist facts and free the guilty. Avery Santos especially—he had watched too many of Barker's carefully built cases dismantled by technicalities or doubt planted at just the right moment.

Beside Barker, Detective Senior Sergeant Hartley made quiet notes in a pocketbook. Older, quieter, Hartley had worked homicides longer than most and still believed the truth usually surfaced if you kept digging. Something about this file had never sat quite right—the victim's work on council development approvals, the timing of certain witness statements—but he kept those thoughts to himself for now.

Avery felt the weight of Barker's stare. He glanced back once, met the detective's eyes, and offered the faintest neutral smile. Barker looked away.

The courtroom clock ticked toward the adjournment.

Justice Bluegum addressed the jury. "The court will adjourn for fifteen minutes. Members of the jury, you are reminded not to discuss the case with anyone, including each other, and to avoid any media coverage or discussion of it. Return at 11:45 am"

"All rise," the associate called as Bluegum stood and left the bench.

The jury filed out. The room exhaled—murmurs rising, reporters typing quickly, family members of the deceased exchanging glances.

Avery stood, buttoned his jacket, and turned to Kristof. "We'll talk more after the break. Hang in there."

Kristof managed a thin smile. "Thanks, mate."

Avery stepped through the bar table gate and into the corridor. The marble echoed under his shoes. Waiting near the lifts, leaning against the wall with casual ease, was Matt "Ollie" Hollander.

Six-three, heavily muscled, long dark hair tied back, Ollie looked more like a frontman for a rock band than a private investigator. But the eyes were sharp, always scanning. He had been Avery's lead investigator—and occasional muscle—for six years now. They had met a decade earlier when Avery, then a rising junior, had got Ollie off drug manufacturing charges. Ollie had used his chemistry degree to "cook" methamphetamine in a shed outside Campbelltown; the police raid had been textbook, but Avery found procedural holes large enough to drive a truck through. Acquittal on all counts. Since then, Ollie had walked the straight line—mostly. He lived on a boat moored at Rozelle Bay, worked cases for Avery, and had never let him down.

Ollie pushed off the wall and handed Avery a takeaway flat white. "How's it going in there?"

"Identification witness folded on distance and lighting," Avery said, taking the coffee. "Crown's still got the forensics to lean on, but we've created space."

Ollie nodded once. "Kristof holding up?"

"Better than most would. He's scared, but he trusts the process—trusts me."

"We heading back to the office now?"

"No, there's no time. Judge wants us back in by 11:45."

Avery and Ollie referred to the café near the courthouse, where they are regulars, as their office. Their actual office was in Phillip Street, in the CBD across from a set of barrister chambers. To distinguish between the two over the years, they'd naturally fallen into the pattern of referring to the café as the office, and their actual office on Phillip Street as chambers. He always found it funny, because even though many barristers encouraged him to be called to the bar and join as a barrister, Avery enjoyed being able to play on both words – that is the world of a solicitor, but still have the skillset to advocate in court.

"Fair enough," Ollie's voice dropped. "Anything else you need before the afternoon session?"

Avery took a sip, considering. "Keep eyes on the usual sources. If any new witnesses surface, I want to know before the Crown does."

"Already running it. Might have something, but I'll get back to you tonight about it"

"Okay, we'll talk later."

Avery glanced back toward the courtroom doors. The trial was only three days in. More Crown evidence ahead: forensics, the knife, the blood spatter expert, perhaps a neighbour or two. Then the defence case—if he could get it admitted without Bluegum shutting down every line of inquiry.

His phone buzzed in his pocket. He ignored it for now.

The associate's voice drifted from inside: "All rise."

Avery straightened his tie. "Back to it."

Ollie gave a small salute. "I'll be here."

Avery walked back toward the doors, composure intact, mind already mapping the next cross-examination.

The courtroom settled once more.

The contest continued.

***

After the exchange with the witness, Ms Ramirez, the remainder of the court that day was relatively straight forward. The prosecutor continued his case with undeniable facts, establishing his case: further eye witnesses establishing that Elle was at home for the entire evening, and no other cars were seen coming or going. The evidence was weak, but did fit nicely in Turner's timeline.

Avery did the count and tally, so far the Prosecution were building their case brick by brick, and he knew that the more bricks they'd build – the bigger hammer he would need to break it all down.

CHAPTER 2 The Informant's Word

THE NEXT MORNING, Courtroom 11 of the Supreme Court of New South Wales felt heavier than the day before. The public gallery was fuller—word had spread through the legal grapevine and the tabloids that the Crown was about to call one of its more controversial witnesses. The air held the faint scent of polished wood, stale coffee from the corridors, and the low buzz of anticipation.

"All rise," the associate intoned as Justice Bluegum entered and took the bench. The jury filed in, some looking more alert than yesterday, others visibly tired from the routine of sequestration rules—no phones, no news, no casual conversations about the case.

Kristof Stanis sat in the dock, shoulders squared but eyes shadowed. He had barely slept; the holding cells at Silverwater Correctional Centre were never kind, and the weight of the previous day's concessions lingered like a bruise. Avery, seated at the defence table, gave his client a brief, steady glance—reassurance without words—before rising to button his jacket as the proceedings resumed.

Crown Prosecutor Elias Turner stood. "Your Honour, the Crown calls Mr Daniel Crowe."

The doors at the side of the courtroom opened. A corrections officer escorted in a man in his late thirties: lean, tattooed forearms visible beneath the sleeves of a plain grey prison-issue tracksuit, hair cropped short, eyes darting briefly around the room before settling on the witness box. Daniel Crowe had spent the last eighteen months at Silverwater on a string of armed robbery and drug possession charges. He walked with the careful gait of someone who knew the system inside out.

Once sworn in, Turner approached the lectern with measured steps.

"Mr Crowe, can you tell the court where you were on the evening of 12 March last year?"

"In Silverwater Remand Centre, C Wing. Same pod as the accused, Kristof Stanis, when he got moved in a few days later. I'd been there about three weeks by then."

"And did you have occasion to speak with Mr Stanis during that time?"

"Yeah. A few times. Blokes talk in there. You pass the hours."

"On or about the night of 15 March—three days after the murder—did Mr Stanis make any statements to you regarding the death of his wife, Elle Stanis?"

Crowe nodded slowly. "Yeah. Late, after lights out. We were in adjacent cells. The walls are thin. He was… upset. Crying, like properly crying. Not just sniffling. Full-on."

Turner let the answer sit for a beat. "What exactly did you hear him say?"

Crowe glanced toward the jury, then back to Turner. "He was saying stuff like, 'How could I do this? How could I do this to her?' Over and over. Then, 'I'm sorry,

Elle. I'm so sorry.' Sounded like he was talking to her, you know? Like she was right there."

A ripple moved through the gallery—soft gasps, quick typing from the press row. Several jurors leaned forward; one woman in the front row pressed her lips together tightly.

Turner continued, voice level. "Did he say anything else that night?"

"Yeah. After a bit he went quiet, then he said, 'I didn't mean for it to go that far.' That's what stuck with me. 'Didn't mean for it to go that far.'"

"Thank you, Mr Crowe." Turner sat.

Avery rose without haste. He had anticipated this witness—jailhouse informants were a Crown staple in circumstantial cases—but the content still landed like a punch. He needed to dismantle it carefully, methodically.

"Mr Crowe," Avery began, tone neutral, almost conversational, "you say this conversation took place after lights out on 15 March. How dark was the cell block at that time?"

"Pitch black, pretty much. Just the emergency lights down the corridor."

"So you couldn't actually see Mr Stanis when he was speaking?"

"No. But I could hear him clear as day. Sound carries."

Avery nodded. "And you were in the cell next to his?"

"Yeah."

"How many other inmates were in that pod that night?"

"Eight, maybe nine. Full house."

"Any of them closer to Mr Stanis's cell than you were?"

Crowe shrugged. "Dunno. Maybe the one on the other side."

"But you're the one who came forward with this information. Why is that?"

"Conscience, I guess. Heard what he said, figured it was important."

Avery tilted his head slightly. "You're currently serving a sentence for armed robbery and possession of a commercial quantity of methamphetamine, correct?"

"Yeah."

"And you have prior convictions for dishonesty offences—three counts of obtaining financial advantage by deception, one for perverting the course of justice?"

Crowe's jaw tightened. "Yeah. Old stuff."

"Old stuff that makes you familiar with how the system works," Avery said mildly. "Including how incentives can be offered to witnesses in custody."

Turner rose. "Your Honour, I object. Counsel is implying without evidence that the witness has been offered any benefit."

"Objection allowed," Bluegum said. "Mr Santos, if you have a basis for suggesting inducement, put it squarely. Otherwise, move on."

Avery accepted the ruling with a small nod. "Mr Crowe, have you applied for a reduction in your sentence or any parole consideration since providing this statement to police?"

"I… yeah, I put in for parole early. Doesn't mean anything was promised."

"But you hope it helps, don't you? A favourable word from the Crown can make a difference."

Crowe hesitated. "I suppose."

Avery let that answer linger. "One more thing. You say Mr Stanis was crying, apologising, saying he didn't mean for it to go that far. Did he ever use the word 'murder'? Or 'kill'? Or 'stab'?"

"No. Not those words."

"Did he confess to stabbing his wife twenty-seven times?"

"No."

"Did he describe how the argument escalated, or what weapon he used?"

"No. Just… the sorry stuff. And the 'didn't mean it to go that far.'"

Avery paused, then: "Mr Crowe, in your experience in prison, do people sometimes talk to themselves at night? Mutter things when they're stressed, grieving, or having nightmares?"

Crowe gave a reluctant nod. "Yeah. Happens all the time."

"So, it's possible Mr Stanis was speaking in his sleep, or grieving out loud, without confessing to anything specific?"

"I guess."

"Thank you." Avery returned to his seat.

The courtroom held its breath for a moment. Turner had no re-examination—nothing to salvage without risking further damage.

Bluegum glanced at the clock. "We'll take the morning tea adjournment now. The court will resume at 11:45 am Members of the jury, the usual reminders apply."

"All rise."

As the jury left, Kristof turned to Avery, voice low. "That hurt."

"It did," Avery admitted. "But he didn't deliver a confession. No specifics. No direct admission. The jury will see it for what it is—a vague, opportunistic statement from a man with every reason to curry favour. We've chipped another piece away."

Kristof exhaled. "Still feels like the noose is tightening."

"It's not," Avery said firmly. "Not while I'm here."

Avery studied Kristof for a beat longer than usual. There was something in the way his client's eyes dropped when he spoke—too quick, too practiced. Avery believed him, or wanted to, but the hesitation lingered like a shadow. Guilt? Shame? Or just grief? He filed it away, said nothing.

***

Avery found Ollie waiting again, this time with two flat whites. He handed one over without a word.

"Snitch?" Ollie asked.

"Classic jailhouse confessor. Thin as paper, but it stings the jury emotionally."

Ollie nodded. "Need me to run anything on him?"

"Quiet check on his parole application timeline and any contact with Barker or the Crown team. Nothing flashy."

"Done."

Avery sipped the coffee, mind already turning to the afternoon: the blood spatter expert was coming soon. Technical, dry, but potentially devastating if not handled right. He wasn't certain he was next, but his years of experience had taught him enough to know how a typical Crown prosecutor executes their case and the strategy they followed. So far, from what he had seen, Avery believed Turner to be a solid prosecutor, but predictable in his processes. He knew better than to be too optimistic about it, but he hoped this predictability of Turner would mean less time focusing on the other side, and more time building his own… And somewhere in the back of his thoughts, Rina lingered there. At least he could see her tonight.

The courtroom doors opened again.

"All rise."

Avery straightened his tie and walked back in.

CHAPTER 3 Notice of Ceasing to Act

THE COURTROOM DAY wrapped at 4:30 pm, the jury dismissed with the standard cautions still echoing. Avery packed his notes methodically, the snitch's testimony lingering like a faint bruise—emotional, but porous enough to poke holes in. Kristof had given him a tired nod before the guards led him away, the kind of quiet gratitude that kept Avery going on days like this.

In the corridor, Ollie waited near the lifts to meet Avery for their traditional after-Court-walk.

"Cheers," Avery said, accepting one. Ollie was drinking his third coffee of the day; the coffee was hot and bitter—perfect. "Snitch did his damage, but we got the vagueness on record. Jury won't hang a man on cell-wall sobs from a guy chasing parole."

Ollie nodded as they started walking. "Crowe's file is clean on explicit deals, but the timing's convenient. Subpoena for lab CCTV on the knife chain gap is drafted—ready when you are."

Avery glanced at him. "Any news on Hale yet?"

Ollie shook his head. "Still nothing fresh. David Hale left the Surry Hills firm a couple of weeks after the withdrawal, nothing with the Law Society. Phone disconnected, email bounces, last address re-let. Quiet exit—no drama on the register, no complaints."

Avery pressed the lift button. "Remind me how we landed the case again."

"Straight handover," Ollie said. "Kristof arraigned in the Supreme Court six weeks after committal. Pleaded not guilty. Hale was still on it then—handled committal, seemed solid. Three days post-arraignment, he files Notice of Ceasing to Act. Cites conflict under the Conduct Rules—Rule 10 or 12, confidential info or former client overlap. Had an emergency mention hearing explaining. Court approves on the papers next day. Hale emails Kristof: 'Unable to continue due to unforeseen conflict. Recommend A. Santos—reputation for difficult acquittals.' Legal Aid NSW took over, until Kristof took us on as representation. Kristof calls chambers that afternoon, we take the brief. File arrives the following week."

Avery stepped into the lift. "And Hale's history with threats?"

"We've gone over it," Ollie replied. "Not much new. Over the years he got the usual: nasty letters from former clients after bad pleas, anonymous calls from inmates claiming he rolled on them for better deals—prison gossip mostly. Changed his number twice, upgraded office security once. Nothing violent, just enough static to make a cautious guy think twice about staying in the game long-term. Could be why he bailed and then faded out—maybe one more threat landed, unrelated to this, and he decided to call it quits."

Avery stared at the floor numbers descending. "Possible. But the referral straight to me, right after arraignment… neat timing."

The lift opened. They stepped out into the late-afternoon light on Phillip Street. "I was thinking back, and I haven't had much contact with Hale myself, which is strange now that I think about it. Especially when I started digging into his cases; he has had some great wins, but some very odd losses too… then there's him dropping the case out of the blue, which is fine, but becoming unreachable afterwards – not normal at all."

Ollie glanced sideways. "You thinking something?"

Avery started drifting, thinking about all previous scenarios he had seen lawyers pull themselves from cases; most of them were due to a major personal impact that most of the time had nothing to do with the case or the client. There was a lawyer, T. Mitchell who dropped all his cases because his wife had died of cancer, and another O'Malley who dropped his case because he was the one with sever health issues – he died 11 months after dropping his cases. But he couldn't recall any circumstances like this.

"Not yet," Avery said. "But check one more angle for me. Any ties between Hale and the Prosecution side— Turner, Crown office staff, even peripheral. Outside the obvious like past cases against each other. Look for bar association events, mutual contacts, anything that isn't just professional collision. Quietly."

Ollie gave a small nod. "Will take a few days to thread without noise. Starting tonight."

"Do it. If it's nothing, fine. But if there's even a faint link, I want it before we close evidence-in-chief."

They parted at the steps—Ollie heading toward the Quay, Avery pulling out his phone. Rina's text from two hours earlier still sat there, unanswered until now: *How you holding up? xx*

He smiled faintly. He remembered months of this—casual conversations at the Anchor when he stopped in after long days, always the same stool near the end of the bar, always the same Lagavulin neat. She'd remembered his order the second time. One night he'd left his business card on the counter—slid it across when paying the tab, maybe on purpose after a particularly draining day, maybe just absent-minded habit. Either way, she'd kept it.

A week later came the first text: *Found this in the tip jar. Figured you left it for a reason. Or I'm reading too much into bar coasters. – Rina*

From then, the flirting had built in quiet increments— texts after tough court days, quick banter when he dropped in, nothing pushed too far.

They had been seeing each other for six months, but lately, after the Stanis case started making headlines, she'd seen him on the court steps once a week just to remind him that his case wasn't his whole life.

Every once in a while, though, he liked to recall how they first began. From that first text message to the eventual regular contact. The messages had grown warmer, more frequent.

He still remembers he had a case that he was losing badly. Yet it was a message from her that kept him happy even though the pressures of being a lawyer sometimes felt like too much. He had messaged her: *Tomorrow night if the jury doesn't bury me first. Anchor, 8?*

Her reply pinged almost instantly: *Deal. I'll save your stool. Bring the winning smile.*

Avery responded to Rina, pocketed the phone and walked toward Circular Quay, the harbour breeze cutting through the day's tension.

CHAPTER 4 THE ANCHOR

AVERY SAT AT the bar waiting for Ollie. This had become a place of comfort for him, not because he is partial to a single malt, but because of its history. He would be consumed by thoughts of cases and strategies more often than not, and when he wasn't with someone, be a client, his partner, colleague or in Court, he made the most of these quiet moments. For that's all they were, just moments. And in these quiet moments, he would like to draw memories of the past. Lately, the memories were of Rina and himself starting. He was taken back to that same bar at the beginning of their relationship–The Anchor. It all felt familiar, almost like déjà vu.

***

The Anchor was quieter mid-week, the after-work rush already easing by 8:05 when Avery pushed through the door. Low lights, brick walls lined with old maritime prints, the soft clink of glasses. Rina was behind the bar, pouring a pint for a regular. She looked up, spotted him sliding onto his usual stool near the end, and her mouth curved into that smile that always seemed to reset his pulse.

"You made it," she said, wiping her hands on a towel and walking over. "Thought the judge might've chained you to the bar table."

"Early adjournment," Avery replied, hanging his jacket on the stool back. "Figured I'd beat the crowd."

She reached for the Lagavulin without asking—neat, generous pour—and set it down with a coaster. "Rough day?"

"Standard murder trial," he said, taking a sip. The peat smoke grounded him. "Client's holding, but the Crown threw an emotional punch today. Jailhouse snitch claiming he heard apologies through the cell wall."

Rina leaned on the bar, elbows propped. "Sounds heavy. You believe the snitch?"

"Not even slightly. Guy's got parole dangling. But juries eat up 'confessions,' even vague ones."

She studied him a beat. "You look like you could use more than whiskey."

He gave a small laugh. "Maybe. How's your night?"

"Steady. Mum's check-up tomorrow—routine. Luca's with his dad tonight."

She stopped there. No quick follow-up, no shift to lighter ground. Instead, her gaze locked on his—green eyes steady, searching, holding him in place. The noise of the bar seemed to drop away: the clink of ice, the low murmur of conversation, the faint hum of the fridge—all of it faded until it was just the two of them, the space between them shrinking without either moving.

The pause stretched, thick with everything they hadn't said over months of bar-side flirting, texts that danced around the edge, his business card she'd kept after he left it on the counter one night (deliberate or absent-minded, he still wasn't sure).

Seconds felt like minutes. Avery felt his pulse kick up, the weight of the day dissolving under the intensity of her stare.

It was an invitation, clear and unguarded. She'd never offered before—not like this.

Avery felt the pull that had been simmering for months finally crest. He'd waited long enough, let the slow burn do its work. Now it was his turn to close the distance.

He leaned forward across the bar, close enough that she could feel his breath. One hand reached out, fingers brushing hers where they rested on the polished wood—light, deliberate. "I've been wanting to do this since the first time you remembered my drink without asking," he said, voice low.

Her breath hitched, lips parting just a fraction. He closed the last inch and kissed her—slow at first, testing, then deeper when she met him halfway, her free hand coming up to curl around the back of his neck. The kiss tasted of whiskey and salt air and months of restraint finally snapping. She pressed forward against the bar edge, soft and sure, and he felt the last of the courtroom tension bleed out of his shoulders.

When they broke apart, foreheads resting together, she let out a small, breathless laugh. "Took you long enough."

"Worth the wait," he murmured.

She reached under the bar, grabbed her keys, and came around without another word. "Shift ends in ten. Stay right there."

Ten minutes later she untied the last knot of her apron, slung her bag over her shoulder, and nodded toward the door.

They stepped out into the cool night. The Rocks streets were quiet, harbour lights shimmering across the water. They walked close—arms brushing, then hands finding each other, fingers lacing without ceremony.

At her door she turned, key already in hand. The streetlamp caught the green in her eyes again, brighter now. She unlocked it, pushed the door open, and looked back at him. "Come inside, Avery."

He followed. The door closed softly behind them.

The flat was small, lived-in—Luca's toys scattered in one corner, a half-finished puzzle on the coffee table, faint lavender from a candle on the kitchen bench. She kicked off her shoes, turned to him, and pulled him toward the hallway without breaking eye contact.

They didn't speak much after that. Clothes shed in a trail from living room to bedroom. Her skin was warm under his hands, her laugh soft against his neck when he found the spot behind her ear that made her shiver. She was unhurried, confident—guiding his hands where she wanted them, whispering his name like it was a secret she'd kept too long.

Later, tangled in sheets that smelled faintly of her shampoo, she traced lazy circles on his chest. "You okay?" she asked quietly.

"Better than okay," he said, pressing a kiss to her temple.

She smiled against his skin. "Good. Because I'm not letting you leave until morning."

He chuckled, low in his throat. "Wouldn't dream of it."

The city hummed faintly outside the window, but in here it was just them—quiet breathing, the slow rhythm of her heartbeat against his. For the first time in weeks, the weight of the trial felt distant.

His phone stayed silent on the nightstand. Tomorrow would bring court again, more witnesses, more pressure. But tonight, he let it wait.

***

He came to when Ollie sat beside him, joining for a drink. They caught up on the speed, and this became almost an unspoken ritual. Before heading into trial, and dangerous waters, they would both meet for a drink before the "big battle." They would continue this ritual until the war, or trial, was over. They both understood their roles and wore them with grace and ease. For Avery, he knew his battle would be in the courtroom like a gladiator in arena. For Ollie, his role was equally important, as his job was outside of the arena, finding weakness in the opposition, tools and weapons for Avery and exerting as much outside pressure as legally possible to assist.

CHAPTER 5 Bloodstain Pattern Analysis

THE MORNING LIGHT filtered through the thin curtains of Rina's bedroom, soft and golden, catching dust motes in lazy spirals. Avery woke first, the unfamiliar weight of someone else's warmth against his side pulling him from sleep. He hadn't stayed over in a few weeks due to late nights at the office. Rina lay curled into him, one arm draped across his chest, her breathing slow and even. Her hair spilled over the pillow, blonde-brown strands catching the sun. For a moment he simply watched her—green eyes closed, face relaxed in a way the bar never allowed—and felt something settle in his chest that hadn't in a long time.

He shifted carefully, not wanting to wake her yet. She stirred anyway, murmuring something incoherent, then opened her eyes and smiled sleepily when she saw him.

"Morning, counsellor," she said, voice husky from sleep.

"Morning." He brushed a strand of hair from her face. "You're right. I should just move out of my place and take permanent residency here. You think the owner will approve."

Avery joked about moving in together frequently, but would has also seriously considered it. He practically lived there these days. He also made the same joke because Rina owns the apartment, and they had lately been discussing whether they both sell their respective places and buy a big house together, or they move into one and rent/sell the other. Semantics. As far as they were concerned, they were both living together, as the only reasons why they'd be apart at nights were on the long office days being pulled away for work.

She laughed quietly, stretching against him. "I don't think she will mind."

They stayed tangled for another twenty minutes—lazy kisses, quiet talk about nothing important: Luca's latest truck obsession, the way Avery hated mornings but loved the smell of coffee brewing, the way she would always wake up to her body-clock's alarm regardless of how late her shift finished. Avery felt the trial clock ticking in the back of his mind but pushed it aside. For once, the courtroom could wait a little longer.

Eventually she rolled out of bed, pulling on an oversized T-shirt that hit mid-thigh. "Coffee?"

"Please."

She padded to the kitchen. He followed a minute later, leaning in the doorway while she measured grounds into the plunger. The flat felt smaller in daylight—lived-in, warm, full of small signs of a life he was only beginning to glimpse.

She handed him a mug. "You've got court today?"

"Blood spatter expert. Crown's going to try to paint the garage like a slaughterhouse."

Rina leaned against the counter, mug cradled in both hands. "And you'll poke holes in it?"

"That's the plan." He took a sip, watched her over the rim. "You okay?"

Her smile was small, genuine. "More than okay. You?"

"Same." He set the mug down, stepped closer, and kissed her forehead. "I'll call you later. After the day's done."

"You better." She rose on her toes, kissed him properly—slow, lingering. "Go win. I love you."

***

He left her flat at 7:45 in the morning, the harbour breeze sharp against his skin as he walked to the Quay and caught a cab to the Supreme Court. By 8:30 he was back in the corridor outside Courtroom 11, tie straightened, mind already shifting gears.

Kristof was already in the dock when Avery entered, escorted in early by the guards. He looked marginally less hollow than yesterday—sleep had helped, or at least dulled the edges—but the strain was still there, etched around his eyes.

Avery took his seat at the defence table, leaned in close while the jury was still filing in. The courtroom wasn't yet full; the associate was busy setting up, the press row half-empty. They had a few minutes.

"Morning," Avery said quietly.

Kristof gave a tired nod. "Morning. Any sleep?"

"Some." Avery kept his voice low. "We need to talk about Elle. The affair."

Kristof's jaw tightened, but he didn't look away. He'd told Avery and Ollie about it weeks ago, during the first full briefing in chambers—Elle had confessed months before her death, said it was a mistake, that she wanted to fix things with him. Kristof had forgiven her, or tried to. They'd been working on it: date nights, counselling, the kids. But the Crown hadn't raised it yet, and Avery had kept it out of opening submissions to avoid giving Turner ammunition.

"I know we've been over it," Avery continued, "but with forensics coming up today—the blood pattern, the knife—Turner might try to spin motive. Jealousy, rage, the classic domestic narrative. If he opens that door, we need to be ready to walk through it our way."

"Okay."

"Now, are you sure you have no idea who she had an affair with? Have you given it more thought? Someone from work? A family-friend? A neighbour? Anything come to mind since we last talked about?"

"No, I knew things were off for a little while, but I didn't know she had an…" Kristof broke off and stared into the distance with both anger and disgust lingering in his eyes. "…an affair. When she first told me I got so angry but I still love her. Loved her. I couldn't think of anyone she could have been with." Kristof sighed with disappointment, "goes to show how much I was paying attention."

Kristof exhaled slowly through his nose. "I didn't kill her, Avery. I knew about the bloke but didn't know who—but only because she told me–didn't know his name, didn't want to. She said it was over. Said she'd ended it the month before… before it happened. We were getting better. I believed her."

Avery studied him. "You never saw him? Never confronted him?"

"No. Elle said he was someone from work—council side, not the site. I trusted her to handle it. Stupid, maybe, but I did."

Avery nodded. "If Turner brings it up, we don't deny it. We own it. You knew, you forgave, you were rebuilding. Shows character, not motive. But if he pushes harder—if he names names or suggests you found out something new that night—we need to know everything. No surprises."

Kristof met his eyes. "There's nothing else. I swear. She was trying to fix things. For the kids, for us. Whoever did this… it wasn't me."

Avery held the gaze a moment longer. The man looked broken, yes, but there was a flicker—something guarded behind the exhaustion, a micro-second where his eyes slid away when he said "I believed her." Avery's instinct prickled. He trusted Kristof's story, but trust wasn't certainty. Not yet. Deep down anyway. On the surface, however, Avery had to act calm and controlled, as always, "I believe you. But belief isn't enough for twelve strangers. Evidence is. So, we keep chipping."

Kristof gave a small, grim smile. "Keep chipping." He was doing his best to hold it together.

The jury began filing in. Avery straightened his tie, turned to face the front as the associate called, "All rise."

Justice Bluegum took the bench. The room settled.

Crown Prosecutor Elias Turner rose. "Your Honour, the Crown calls Dr. Elena Vasquez, forensic scientist specialising in bloodstain pattern analysis."

Dr. Vasquez entered from the side door—mid-forties, dark hair pulled into a neat bun, white lab coat over a navy suit. She carried herself with the calm authority of someone who spent her days explaining violence through physics and geometry. She took the oath and the stand without flourish.

Turner began with the basics: qualifications (PhD in forensic biology, fifteen years at the NSW Forensic Lab, hundreds of crime scenes), then moved to the Stanis garage.

"Dr. Vasquez, you examined the crime scene at the Marrickville residence on 13 March last year?"

"Yes. I attended at approximately 4:00 am, after initial scene preservation."

"Describe the bloodstain patterns you observed."

Vasquez gestured to the large photographs projected on the screen—garage floor, walls, the knife. "The victim sustained twenty-seven stab wounds, primarily to the torso and neck. The majority were delivered with force, creating high-velocity spatter on the walls and ceiling consistent with repeated thrusting motions. Cast-off patterns on the ceiling suggest the attacker was standing over the victim, swinging the knife upward and outward."

She pointed to a close-up. "Here, on the lower wall, we see medium-velocity spatter—likely from arterial breaches—mixed with contact stains where the victim's body was in contact with the surface. The distribution indicates the attack occurred near the centre of the garage floor, with the victim attempting to move away, creating wipe marks and drag patterns."

Turner let the images sink in. Jurors shifted uncomfortably; one woman in the back row covered her mouth.

"And the knife?" Turner asked.

"Recovered from the scene, handle and blade both bloodied. The blood on the handle was primarily the victim's, with transfer patterns consistent with an overhand grip—fingers wrapped around it tightly. Prints on the handle matched the accused."

Kristof exhaled sharply beside Avery.

Turner finished with the motive angle. "In your opinion, Dr. Vasquez, does the pattern suggest a frenzied, emotional attack?"

"I object, Counsel is leading the witness." Avery rose, knowing it wouldn't to much good. He knew that Turner would rephrase and get the same answer from the witness anyway.

"Let me rephrase. What does the pattern suggest to you, in your expert opinion, Dr. Vasquez?" Directed Turner.

Vasquez nodded once. "The number of wounds, the depth, the distribution of spatter—all consistent with an attack driven by intense emotion rather than a controlled execution. Rage, perhaps, or panic. Generally, these are referred to as crimes of passion."

"Thank you." Turner sat.

Avery rose slowly. He didn't rush. He walked to the lectern, let the silence stretch just long enough to pull the jury's attention.

"Dr. Vasquez," he began, voice calm, "you described high-velocity spatter on the ceiling. Consistent with repeated thrusting. But also consistent with defensive wounds, correct? If the victim was fighting back, raising her arms, the knife could strike bone or create the same upward cast-off?"

Vasquez considered. "Yes… possible. But the volume and distribution lean toward offensive action."

"Possible, though," Avery repeated. "And the wipe marks and drag patterns—could those indicate someone attempting to move the body after the attack? Staging, perhaps?"

"Could be," she conceded. "Or the victim trying to crawl away."

Avery moved to the projected photo of the knife handle. "The prints on the handle. You said they matched Mr Stanis. But the blood on the handle—was it wet or dry when the prints were made?"

"Wet. Fresh transfer."

"So, the prints could have been made after the attack—someone picking up the knife in the aftermath, not necessarily during?"

Vasquez paused. "Theoretically, yes. But the grip pattern is consistent with use."

"Theoretically," Avery echoed. "Now, Doctor, you've seen the photographs of the witness and his clothing of the night of the incident. The blood spatter on the accused's clothing—minimal on the front, correct? No high-velocity spatter on his upper body, clothing or face."

"That's correct."

"Odd for someone who allegedly stabbed another person twenty-seven times at close range, wouldn't you say?"

"It's unusual," Vasquez admitted. "But he could have changed clothes or cleaned up."

"Could have," Avery said. "Or he could have arrived after the fact, found his wife, picked up the knife in shock. No spatter because he wasn't the attacker."

Turner rose. "Objection—speculative."

"Objection allowed," Bluegum said. "Mr Santos, questions, not argument."

Avery nodded. "No further questions."

He returned to his seat. Kristof leaned in. "Was that good or bad?"

"It chipped," Avery murmured. "We keep chipping."

The morning session ended. Bluegum adjourned for lunch. Avery stood, mind already turning to the pathologist after the break—and the conversation he needed to have with Kristof about the affair again. Turner hadn't touched it yet, but the motive door was cracking open.

***

As expected by Avery, Ollie waited with fresh coffee ready for their walk to the office.

"Blood spatter?" Ollie asked.

"Managed," Avery said. "But Turner's building to something. We need to talk to Kristof about the affair again—make sure there's nothing he hasn't told us. And your check on Hale?"

"Still threading. One small thing—Hale and Turner were both on a panel at a bar association seminar two years ago. 'Ethics in Criminal Practice.' Nothing dramatic, but they shared a stage. Could be coincidence."

Avery's eyes narrowed. "Or not. Keep digging."

Ollie nodded. "On it."

Avery glanced at his phone—no messages from Rina yet. He smiled faintly, pocketed it, and headed back toward the courtroom.

CHAPTER 6 THE PATHOLOGIST

THE AFTERNOON SESSION reconvened at 2:15 pm
Courtroom 11 had grown warmer, the air thick with the
scent of polished timber and the faint metallic tang of
tension. Jurors returned to their seats with the weary
focus of people who had already seen too much blood in
photographs. Kristof sat rigid in the dock, hands folded,
eyes fixed on the bar table as if willing the evidence to
change shape.

Justice Bluegum settled onto the bench. "The Crown
may proceed."

Elias Turner rose. "Your Honour, the Crown calls Dr.
Hale—no relation to the former solicitor, Dr. Marcus
Hale," he added with a small, dry smile that drew a few
chuckles from the press row. "Dr. Hale is the forensic
pathologist who conducted the post-mortem
examination on Elle Stanis."

Dr. Hale entered—late fifties, wiry build, wire-
rimmed glasses, the calm detachment of a man who had

opened hundreds of bodies and still slept at night. He took the oath and the stand with quiet efficiency.

Turner began with credentials: board-certified, 22 years at the NSW Institute of Forensic Medicine, testified in over 450 homicide cases, published on perimortem trauma and wound patterns in domestic violence. Then he moved to the findings.

"Dr .Hale, describe the injuries you observed."

Hale spoke clearly. "The victim sustained twenty-seven stab wounds. Twenty-one penetrated vital structures—heart, lungs, major vessels. Defensive injuries on hands and forearms were superficial; she attempted to block or grab the blade but was quickly overpowered. Cause of death was exsanguination compounded by cardiac tamponade. The weapon was consistent with the recovered kitchen knife—single-edged, serrated, approximately 20 cm blade."

Turner projected autopsy photographs—clinical, merciless. Jurors shifted; one woman in the back row pressed a tissue to her mouth.

"In your expert opinion and experience, what does the number and nature of the wounds indicate the attack?"

Hale's tone remained clinical but firm. "The excessive number of wounds—far beyond what is required to cause death—is a hallmark of personal animus. The clustering around the chest and abdomen shows intent to kill, not merely to incapacitate. The force, repetition, and targeting are consistent with rage or explosive emotion, commonly seen in intimate-partner homicides where betrayal or jealousy is a factor. I have documented this pattern in numerous cases involving spouses or partners, particularly when infidelity is involved."

The jury were attentive and listening, following a light gasp of shock as if they were drawing the conclusion that Elle was having an affair and that was the motive for Kristof to kill her.

My client was losing this case. Avery thought to himself.

Turner paused to let the jury absorb it. "And the time of death window?"

"Body temperature, rigor mortis, and livor mortis place death between 10:30 pm and midnight on 12 March. The progression aligns closely with the reported argument heard by neighbours around 10:45 pm"

"Thank you." Turner sat.

Avery rose. He approached the lectern knowing this witness was a fortress—calm, credentialed, unshakable.

"Dr. Hale," he began evenly, "the defensive wounds were superficial. Could that indicate the victim was restrained quickly, limiting her resistance?"

Hale nodded slightly. "Possible. But the presence of any defensive injury shows she was conscious and resisting for at least part of the attack. The superficial nature suggests the attacker quickly gained control."

Avery tried the absence of injury on Kristof. "You examined the accused. No cuts, no bruises on his hands or arms. Does that exclude him as the attacker?"

"No," Hale said firmly. "Absence of injury on the accused is not unusual. The attacker can avoid self-injury by controlling the victim's arms, using clothing, or simply being stronger. It does not rule him out."

Avery moved to the timeline. "The time of death window—10:30 pm to midnight. Mr Stanis's alibi places him at a pub until 11:15 pm, with witnesses and footage. Given what you have already stated, you're also stating that the death could have occurred during the very time my client was at the pub with witnesses and footage placing him there?"

A slight slip up from the Prosecution, he just missed it.

Hale met his eyes. "The window is an estimate based on physical signs. I cannot exclude later death, but the body temperature drop and rigor progression align more closely with the later part of that range—towards midnight."

Avery felt the jury shift—Hale's calm certainty was landing. He had no more ground to gain without risking overreach.

But the jury didn't know what Avery knew, he may have just walked Hale into a trap, and even Turner if it goes to plan.

"Dr. Hale, so at first you say under oath that it the window is between 10:30 pm to midnight… then you say it's actually between 11 pm to midnight? Are you changing your testimony now that you have been told about my client's whereabouts during the earlier portion of that window?"

"I object, Your Honour. Counsel is introducing facts not yet established in evidence." It wasn't missed this time.

"Objection allowed. The jury will disregard the timeline of the defendant's alibi."

"Your Honour," Avery was up, "my client does have an alibi for the time of the murder, and there are corroborating witnesses and video footage showing him completely somewhere else during the presumed time of death – I have a right to explore these circumstances whilst Dr. Hale is on the stand."

"You will have that right when it is your turn to present your case, Mr Santos, but you will be prohibited from presenting them during this line of questioning, if you haven't yet established them as evidence in this Court.:

"Of course, Your Honour. I will do."

It worked. Even though, the alibi hadn't yet been introduced to the jury by the defence, that seed had now been planted. Furthermore, by arguing with the judge about when Avery could introduce it doesn't necessarily change the fact that it exists. On top of that, Avery slipped another under the cover – when he said *my client does have an alibi for the time of the murder*, even though the alibi was only for the earlier period of time.

"Dr. Hale. What was the time of the murder again, as you stated in your earlier testimony and medical examiner report?"

"Between 10:30 pm to midnight."

"Thank you. Nothing further" Avery returned to his seat.

Kristof leaned in, voice low. "He hurt us when it looked like you jumped the gun there."

Avery nodded. "Jury heard rage, personal motive, timeline matching the argument. We chipped, but I played something too, you'll see."

The session ended at 4:00 pm Bluegum adjourned until morning. As the jury filed out, Avery caught Barker's stare from the gallery—harder today, almost satisfied. Barker looked away first with a chuffed yet disgusted smile.

Avery gathered his notes, exchanged a quick word with Kristof—"We're still in the fight"—then stepped through the bar table gate into the corridor. The usual post-session hum filled the space: reporters typing, family members whispering, clerks moving files.

He didn't see Barker until the detective stepped directly into his path.

Jacob Barker stood with arms folded, blocking the way to the lifts. No uniform today—just a dark jacket over a shirt and tie—but the posture was pure police: shoulders squared, jaw set, eyes locked on Avery like a target. Up close, the grey in his temples caught the fluorescent light, and the handsome face was twisted into something harder.

"Mr Santos," Barker said, voice low enough not to carry far but sharp enough to cut. "Got a minute?"

Avery stopped, met the stare without flinching. "Detective. Something on the record?"

Barker's lip curled. "Off the record. Just wanted to say it to your face. You defence lawyers—scum of the earth. You stand there in your tailored suits, picking apart good police work, planting doubt where there shouldn't be any. A woman's dead, twenty-seven times stabbed in her own garage, her kids left without a mother, and you're out here trying to sell the jury she was killed by a ghost or some phantom lover. You make me sick."

Avery kept his expression neutral, voice calm and even. "I'm doing my job, Detective. The same as you. The evidence has to hold up. If it doesn't, that's not my fault—it's the system working the way it's supposed to."

Barker stepped closer, voice dropping to a near-growl. "Your job is to get scum off. Kristof Stanis is no different from the rest of them. You'll twist every fact, every witness, until the jury can't see straight. But I was there. I saw the blood. I saw her body. And I'll be damned if I let you walk a wife-killer out the door because you're good at sleight of hand and reasonable doubt."

Avery held the gaze, unflinching. "If the evidence is as strong as you say, Detective, you've got nothing to worry about. The jury will see it. Unless there's something else you're worried they'll see instead."

Barker's eyes narrowed, a muscle ticking in his jaw. "Watch yourself, Santos. People like you don't always come out on top. One day the truth catches up."

He turned sharply and walked away, shoulders tense, a firm but slightly limped step in his pace – resembling either a wound or injury sustained many years back; disappearing around the corner toward the witness waiting area.

Avery exhaled slowly, the corridor noise rushing back in. He was used to seeing detectives all bent out of shape with an obvious disdain towards defence lawyers – however, most of the time, it would be the product of an officer or detective being interrogated thoroughly or embarrassed on the stand by a criminal defence lawyer. He thought it was strange, how much animosity Barker had towards him, especially considering they'd never encountered each other before. Was it because he found the victim as lead detective on scene? Was it because he hated my client? Was it a cop thing? These questions circled his mind until he felt a firm tap on his shoulder. Ollie appeared at his side a moment later, coffee in hand, having caught the tail end from a few metres away.

"Heard the tone," Ollie said quietly. "Barker's rattled."

"He's personal," Avery replied, voice low. "That wasn't just frustration. That was something else. That was fear. He's invested—too invested for a clean investigation."

Ollie handed him the flat white. "Hale call still the strongest thread. Timing's too perfect for coincidence."

Avery took a sip. "If Barker's this invested, there's more under the surface. And when we find it, we don't accuse—we prove."

Ollie nodded. "I'll have the tender files by tonight. Elle's last submissions—council records are public. If Barker or anyone close to him touched them, it'll show."

Avery's phone buzzed. Rina: *Survived another day? Call when you're free. Miss the sound of your voice already xxx*

He smiled faintly. "Yeah. Got somewhere to be."

Avery then noticed and watched Barker disappear around the corner, then turned back toward the lifts.

Kristof's thin smile from earlier replayed in his mind—the way his client had looked away when Avery mentioned the affair again. Belief was one thing; certainty was another. Avery believed Kristof hadn't killed Elle. But he couldn't shake the quiet feeling that his client was still holding something back. Something small, perhaps. Something that could matter.

Ollie raised an eyebrow. "So, you two getting married yet or what?"

Avery snapped back to reality, but didn't answer, just clapped him on the shoulder with a smile and walked toward the lifts.

***

Arriving at Rina's place felt like gravity had been turned off. He relished in the fact that he felt the weight of the world float off his shoulders whenever he was around her. He loved that. He knew that in the outside world, the battle would rage on, but in the quiet confines of this space – he could relax and just simply be free.

Outside though, the day was done. But the shadows were lengthening.

70

CHAPTER 7 Occam's Razor

THE COURTOOM FELT smaller that morning, the air denser, as if the walls themselves had absorbed the previous days' testimony and now pressed it back out. The public gallery was packed — reporters squeezed shoulder-to-shoulder, Elle's sister in the front row clutching a tissue, a handful of council colleagues who had taken leave to attend. The jury entered looking heavier-eyed, their notebooks already thick with notes. Kristof sat in the dock with the stillness of a man who had decided not to fight the current anymore, only to endure it.

Justice Bluegum settled onto the bench. "The Crown may proceed."

Elias Turner rose, his usual measured calm edged with something sharper today. He had saved one of his strongest cards for near the end of evidence-in-chief.

"Your Honour, the Crown calls Detective Senior Sergeant Paul Hartley."

Hartley entered from the side door—mid-fifties, greying buzz-cut, the quiet solidity of a man who had spent thirty years in the job without ever raising his voice in public. He was Barker's second on the investigation: scene attendance, witness coordination, the formal interview with Kristof the morning after the body was found. He took the oath with the same understated precision he brought to every report he filed.

Turner began with the basics.

"Detective Senior Sergeant Hartley, you were the co-lead investigator with Detective Barker. You attended the crime scene at approximately 4:15 am on 13 March last year?"

Avery was paying close attention to the detail looking for any loose threads, or chinks in the armour. He knew the processes all too well – it would be common procedure for the patrols and general police to be dispatched first, followed by other emergency services required from ambulance to fire services, then detectives and forensics to arrive up to hours later. He knew all this, and so far the timeline fine; however, it was his job to pay close attention. It was his job to make sure.

"Yes." Hartley responded.

"And later that morning, did you conduct a formal interview with the accused, Kristof Stanis, at Marrickville Police Station?"

"Yes. Commenced at 9:47 am Mr Stanis was cautioned, declined legal representation at that stage, and agreed to be interviewed."

Turner tendered the interview recording and transcript as exhibits. The courtroom screens flickered to life with still images: Kristof in the interview room, unshaven, eyes red-rimmed, a paper cup of water untouched in front of him.

Turner moved straight to the heart of it.

"Detective, during that interview, did Mr Stanis make any statements regarding his relationship with the deceased?"

Hartley nodded. "He confirmed they had been married twelve years, two children. He said things had been strained for about eight months. When asked why, he stated—and I quote—'Elle told me that six months ago she'd started an affair. She said it was a mistake, that it was over for about a month, and we were working on things. Counselling, trying to get back on track for the kids.'"

A soft ripple moved through the gallery. Kristof's jaw clenched visibly; his hands, resting on his knees, tightened until the knuckles blanched.

Turner leaned in slightly. "Did he elaborate on how he felt about the affair?"

Hartley's voice remained level, but he delivered the words with deliberate weight. "He said he was 'furious at first.' He repeated that several times—'furious,' 'hurt,' 'betrayed.' When I asked if the anger had lingered, he said, 'It ate at me. Every time I looked at her, I saw him. Some bloke she wouldn't name. Late nights, excuses, the way she'd shut her phone when I walked in.' He admitted he'd confronted her more than once. Said he'd asked her point-blank who it was, and she'd shut it down every time. 'It doesn't matter anymore,' she told him. But he didn't believe that. He said, 'I kept thinking, how do you just switch it off? How do you go back to normal after someone else has been inside your marriage?'"

Avery could have objected, but the jury were already thinking it anyway. *Now is not the time to fight back yet*, he thought to himself. The affair happened, there was no way around it. He knew they would have their chance to provide their side, but for now they had to brace it.

The jury leaned forward almost as one. A woman in the second row pressed a hand to her chest; the man beside her stopped writing and stared at the dock.

Turner pressed on. "Did Mr Stanis say anything about the night of the murder in relation to the affair?"

Hartley glanced toward Kristof for the briefest second. "He claimed he was at the pub until 11:15 pm, got home after midnight, found her in the garage. But when I asked if the affair had come up again that evening—if there had been any argument about it—he paused for a long time. Then he said, 'We'd been arguing on and off about it for weeks. She kept saying it was finished. I kept saying I needed to know who. That night… I don't remember exactly what was said. It was heated. But I didn't hurt her.'"

"I object, Your Honour. Hearsay."

The Judge disallowed the objection.

Turner let the silence stretch. "In your experience as a homicide detective, Detective Hartley, does the pattern of twenty-seven stab wounds, the frenzied nature of the attack as described by the pathologist and bloodstain analyst, align with the kind of emotional state Mr Stanis described?"

"Your Honour, I object. Counsel is leading again."

"Objection allowed. Please rephrase Mr Turner."

"Detective, in your experience, what conclusion did you draw from the stab wounds?"

Hartley didn't hesitate. "Yes. In my thirty years, I've seen this exact pattern in domestic homicides where infidelity is the trigger. The excessive number of wounds, the clustering around the heart and chest—it's not clinical. It's personal. It's rage. The kind of rage that builds when a man feels his family, his whole life, has been stolen from him by someone else. Crimes of passion. They don't look like calculated murder. They look like this."

A murmur ran through the gallery—soft gasps, quick typing from the press row. Several jurors exchanged glances; one older man shook his head slowly.

Turner finished quietly. "Thank you, Detective. One more question, looking at these facts and evidence, did it present Mr Stanis as guilty of these charges?"

"Objection. Leading."

"Question withdrawn. No further questions." Turner withdrew before the judge could provide any direction.

Avery rose without haste. He walked to the lectern, letting the heavy silence settle before he spoke.

"Detective Senior Sergeant Hartley," he began, voice calm and even, "you've described Mr Stanis as 'furious,' 'hurt,' 'betrayed.' Those are his words from the interview, correct?"

"Yes."

"And he also said, multiple times, that the affair was over, that they were in counselling, that he loved his wife and was committed to fixing things for their children?"

Hartley nodded reluctantly. "He said those things too."

"Did he ever say he wanted revenge? Or that he intended to confront the other man?"

"No."

"Did he ever threaten Elle, or say he couldn't live with what she'd done?"

"No."

The Detective was experienced. He knew not to give anything away. It was a typical expectation; cops would overshare in evidence-in-chief for the Prosecution, and under share in cross. Or rather, they would usually answer more than what was asked of them to help the Prosecution, and barely answer a syllable when answering the defence questions.

Avery moved to the key gap. "In the interview, when you pressed him on whether the affair had come up that final night, he said he didn't remember exactly what was said. But he maintained he didn't hurt her. You have no recording of him confessing to any violence?"

"Correct. No confession."

"No admission that he knew the other man's identity?"

"He said he didn't know the name. Only suspicions."

"And no forensic evidence—no messages, no calls, no witnesses—placing Mr Stanis with knowledge of the man's identity in the hours before the murder?"

Hartley paused. "Not that we located in the initial extraction. Later analysis showed no direct threats or accusations to any third party."

"Thank you." Avery paused, then: "One last thing. In your experience with crimes of passion, Detective, is it common for the perpetrator to leave the weapon at the scene, covered in their own fingerprints, rather than dispose of it?"

Hartley's mouth tightened. "It happens. Shock sets in after the act. They panic, drop it, run."

"Or…" Avery said mildly, "someone else leaves it there. Someone who wants it to look personal."

Turner rose. "Objection—speculative."

"Objection allowed," Bluegum said. "Mr Santos, questions only."

"Detective, I will rephrase. If it looked like someone was to frame my client, isn't it possible that someone else could have committed this crime the exact way it has been presented?"

"It is possible, though Occam's Razor says otherwise. It is usually the simplest explanation presented, which is the correct one."

"You're right Detective, most of the time it is. However, isn't there the chance that it was committed by someone else wanting to frame my client. I am not asking if it is likely it happened. I am not asking if you think that's happened. Just given the fact that there's a lack of physical evidence placing my client at the crime scene at the time of the death, isn't it possible it could have been someone else."

"Anything is possible. But-"

Avery cut him off and nodded. "No further questions."

He returned to his seat. Kristof leaned in, voice low and shaky. He attempted to speak, but nothing came out.

"Don't worry, this is all part of it." Avery murmured. "He attacked and attacked, which is normal. But he didn't deliver a smoking gun. No confession. No proof you knew who. The jury heard passion, but they also heard doubt. We keep fighting."

Bluegum glanced at the clock. "We'll take the morning adjournment. Resume after lunch."

As the jury filed out, Avery caught Barker's stare from the gallery—cold, almost triumphant. Hartley stepped down and walked past the bar table, eyes forward.

***

In the corridor Ollie was waiting, slim folder in hand, expression tight.

"Got it," Ollie said quietly, passing the folder. "Elle's final council submission—the one she was finishing the week she died. Development consent for the Marrickville project. Fast-tracked despite objections. She had actually denied this submission previously. Twice. This time, signed off 15 February—four weeks before the murder."

Avery flipped it open. The signature stared back: Elle Stanis, Assessment Officer.

Ollie continued. "But look at this." Ollie handed flipped to other pages. "This is Elle's signature. And so

82

are these." Ollie pointed to different sets that do not seem matching, even though they are legible enough to sign the same name.

"Someone forged to get this tender approved. Who was it for again?"

"Greyrock Developments—haven't found anything on them. Largest development organisation in the country, and top three in the Oceania region. Director is squeaky clean too, or at least on the surface."

"What else?"

"There's something a little too convenient. I haven't been able to unravel yet. But the first tender was denied approximately eight months prior to finally getting approved."

"What does that have to do with anything?"

"Well, I remember what you told me about stepping back and looking at the big picture. Look at this timeline."

Ollie pointed to the documents, and then opened up Avery's notes. Inside the main legal pad (he always had one master pad for all the basic notes and key entries of a case he was on), was the timeline page detailing what he knew about the case specifically.

Avery's tone changed with a sense of slight discovery. "You could be right. First tender gets denied eight months earlier. Same time, Elle and Kristof's marriage are on the rocks – for who knows how long that had been. But she starts an affair just two months later, which also happens to be when the next tender gets denied. Then all of a sudden, tender gets approved one month later, which falls in line with the supposed time that she ends her affair."

"Before you ask, no I haven't been able to find anything on the affair."

"That's okay. We need another angle instead. Instead of trying to find who she was having an affair with, let's look into Greyrock and see if you can dig any personal link between employees, workers, contractors or outside personnel, even if they have nothing to do with the Marrickville project. There's usually a trail somewhere."

"On it. Anything else on Greyrock whilst I am looking into it?"

Avery closed the folder. "Elle flagged irregularities. She was about to deny the offer again, and whoever it is who signed her signature either killed her or knew of it. If she talked, the whole thing collapses. Greyrock loses millions, if not more. It sure looks like Greyrock – but don't know yet what the affair has to do with it, even though the timing seems a little too coincidental."

Ollie's voice dropped. "This isn't jealousy. It's a clean-up. Dressed up as a crime of passion."

Kristof was escorted past. He caught Avery's eye, raised a questioning brow.

Avery gave a small, firm nod. "We're not putting you in the box, mate. You stay silent. They're the ones who have to answer now."

Kristof exhaled, shoulders dropping a fraction in relief.

Avery pocketed the folder. His phone buzzed—Rina: *Survived the morning? Thinking of you.*

He typed back: *Closer than yesterday. See you tonight. Got something real.*

Her reply: *Door's open. Whiskey's waiting. Tell me everything.*

He slipped the phone away and turned back toward the courtroom doors.

The Crown still had witnesses left—phone data, perhaps a neighbour hearing some commotion, perhaps Elle's best friend—but the ground had shifted beneath the surface. The jury didn't see it yet.

But Avery did.

CHAPTER 8 The Best Friend

THE AFTERNOON LIGHT slanted through the high windows of Courtroom 11, turning dust motes into tiny sparks and casting long shadows across the bar table. The jury had returned from the adjournment looking more guarded than ever—notebooks open, pens poised, faces set in the quiet determination of people who knew the end of the Crown's case was near.

Turner stood at the lectern, tie perfectly knotted, voice steady but carrying the weight of finality.

"Your Honour, the Crown calls Ms Sophie Laurent."

Sophie Laurent entered—mid-forties, dark hair pulled into a neat chignon, eyes already glistening. Elle's closest friend since university, a senior planner at the same council department. She took the oath with a small tremble in her hand.

Turner wasted no time.

"Ms Laurent, how long had you known Elle Stanis?"

"Twenty years. We started at the council together. She was my best friend."

"And in the months leading up to March last year, did Elle confide in you about difficulties in her marriage?"

Sophie nodded, swallowing hard. "Yes. About two months before… she told me she'd had an affair. In the grand scheme of things she said it was brief. A mistake. She said she ended it because she loved Kristof and the kids. She was devastated she'd hurt him."

Turner let the jury absorb that. "Did she tell you who the other man was?"

"No. She refused. Said it would only make things worse if Kristof ever found out. She was scared—not of violence, but of losing him completely. She said he was already so angry, so hurt. He kept asking who it was. She kept saying it didn't matter anymore."

A soft sob escaped her. She pressed a tissue to her mouth.

"Did you observe any changes in Elle's behaviour during that time?"

"She was withdrawn. Cried a lot when we talked on the phone. She told me Kristof would glare at her phone sometimes, ask who she was texting. Once she showed me a message from him—'We need to talk about this tonight.' She was terrified he'd push until he got a name."

Turner moved closer to the witness box. "On the evening of 12 March, did Elle contact you?"

"Yes. A text at 8:42 pm *'He's asking again. I don't know what to say'* That was the last one I got from her."

The Court allowed Turner to exhibit a screenshot of the phone conversation showing Elle had texted Sophie at 8:42pm that evening, stating *'He's asking again. I don't know what to say.'*

"And what do you think this was referring to, Ms Laurent?"

"Objection, Your Honour, that's hearsay." Avery stood.

"Your Honour, the witness had shared a deep relationship with the victim, who openly confided in her as seen by the witness' testimony and evidence presented, I think the witness should be allowed to share her observations due to her circumstances with the victim at that time."

"Overruled. Question allowed, the witness may answer." The judge said.

"What do you think Elle was talking about when she messaged you, Ms Laurent?"

"What she was always talking about. Kristof asking who the affair was with again."

The gallery inhaled sharply. Kristof's head bowed lower; his shoulders rose and fell in silent rhythm. "I don't remember texting her that night" Kristof whispered to Avery adamantly.

Avery, looking confused and unsure what to do with that information knew he was playing with fire if he approached this plan the way he intended. There's a rule in cross-examination, never ask a question you don't already know the answer to.

"Are you absolutely certain you didn't text her that night?" Avery looked Kristof directly in the eyes, whilst whispering with certainty.

He quickly scanned the evidence pages submitted to him before the Prosecution months earlier, looking through both Kristof's phone records and Elle's. He found it. There were no messages that night in evidence on Kristof's phone sent to Elle, other than one at 4:58 pm stating "We are clocking off early, I will be home after a few drinks with the guys, they smashed the finish today."

There was a text message that was received on Elle's phone at 8:31pm that evening saying "we need to talk", but it wasn't from Kristof's number nor any number that had shown up in Elle's phone. There was no history about it. Avery just remembered that forensics were still supposed send through their findings to see if it can be uncovered. They were too slow and taking too long, so he had just recalled he'd added it on Ollie's to-do list weeks prior. He made a mental note to check in on its progress. There were also pages with some highlighted text conversations with what seem to be from her former lover, which were from different dates and timestamps, with a new number rotating every month or so. Messages such as "meet me at the hotel tonight at 8" or "same place same time". It was obvious to everyone who'd seen the discovery that these were affair text message exchanges, but there wasn't much else to them, particularly as they started to die off matching the supposed timeline of Elle breaking it off a month prior.

There were only three messages, all from unknown and untraceable numbers saying *"Call me"* received six weeks prior to Elle's death, *"Elle, this is serious, I am sorry but let me explain."* sent two weeks prior, and then the message *"we need to talk"* sent on the night of her death. Avery already believed that these random sporadic messages had to have been from her former lover, and Ollie had still been unsuccessful in tracing the source, so he parked it. he didn't know what to make of it until now.

"I object, Your Honour. That is hearsay and has not been admitted into evidence."

"I have already overruled, counsellor. Please continue Mr Turner."

Turner finished quietly. "Thank you, Ms Laurent."

Avery rose. He approached slowly, voice soft but clear.

"Ms Laurent, Elle told you the affair was over, correct?"

"Yes."

"And that she wanted to save her marriage? That she loved Kristof and the children?"

"Absolutely. She was doing everything—counselling, date nights, talking to the kids about family time. She was committed."

"When did she end the affair?"

"About two months prior."

"You're saying she ended it two months prior to when she was killed?"

"I already answered that. Yes."

"Did she tell you that she had started up with him again?"

"No. She didn't and I would have known if she did."

This was the risky part.

"Then when didn't you tell the Court and the jury about the times when Elle told you she had been receiving messages from *him*… and I am not referring to my client. But the same *him* she had been having an affair with."

"Objection! Counsel is testifying and there is no evidence to his claims! Your Honour!"

"Your Honour, I have a right to question the witness based on her the fact that she had shared a deep connection with the victim."

"Yes, you do have that right Mr Santos, but you cannot testify to what hasn't been presented with the evidence in Court."

Avery bluffed, but he knew this would play in his favour. "Absolutely, Your Honour, however I am just going to ask the witness about her communications with the victim, and the evidence I will refer to has already been presented in Court, as I am only using the victim's phone records."

"Overruled. You may proceed Mr Santos."

"Ms Laurent, can you tell the Court how many times Elle spoke to you about reconciling with her lover, after their apparent split two months prior." At the same time as questioning, Avery didn't make too much eye-contact but instead was looking at the phone records whilst waiting for Sophie to answer. This was a cheap tactic, but often deployed the desired outcome by sheer distraction. Instead of asking the witness to verify something, you ask them to confirm something else but assuming the original question was already assumed. In this case, by assuming Elle had been considering reconciling with her lover it no longer draws attention to whether or not Sophie knew, but how many times did Elle tell her about it; or at least that's what Avery thought.

"She never said she was reconciling with him. Only that he wanted to after they initially stopped. She was torn because she loved Kristof but also let herself get caught up on the romance of her affair."

"I see you rarely spoke about it over text," Avery was standing with folder in hand looking through the Elle's phone records and message conversations with Sophie, "but it did look like she would message you something like 'let's talk' or 'I spoke to him today' followed by a long phone conversation. Is this how your communication would typically be between you two?"

"Yes, generally the messages were short as we were both busy with work, and we also had work phones, by working for the government. But most of the time for actual talk we would have a real phone conversation."

"And these conversations would be about everything? From work, to her husband and family, and to her lover and affair?"

"Yes, like I said she was my best friend and she could come to me for anything."

"Right, so that would explain the calls after her lover tried to get back with her four weeks prior to her death, six weeks prior to her death, then two weeks prior to her death, isn't that what you just said?"

Avery was attempting to blur the lines, but he was right in where he was heading.

"Yes, she called me after each of those times."

"It looks like she would message you first, then call, like you testified earlier." Avery was allowed to present the text messages between Elle and Sophie as evidence to the Court, "for example, here her former lover would text her, then she texted you on this Thursday night saying *'guess who tried to contact me'*, and then four weeks later, *'he did it again, I will call you tonight about it.'* Does that sound right to you?"

"Yes, it does."

"So, when she messaged you that night saying *'He's asking again. I don't know what to say'* did you end up speaking to her about her former lover?" It was another trap. Avery had already walked her down the path;

whatever she answers here only helps Avery's case and hurts Sophie's testimony as it would paint her to misconstrue the truth on the stand in her earlier testimony if she tried to deny it, all whilst planting the seed of doubts with the jury.

"I did not end up speaking to her that night." Sophie grabbed a tissue again as she recalled that night being the night of Elle's death.

Avery had won some logic points, but sometimes the emotional points are too hard to combat against. He could see the jury still feeling the pain of Sophie. He had to quickly adapt.

"Now, I know you lost your best friend that night. And you truly have my condolences." Avery was about take another risk. "But given what you know about Elle trying to reconcile things, and Kristof trying to forgive her and rebuild with her… I know you want justice for your friend, but I want you to think about all the evidence here and the facts beyond that – isn't it possible that someone else did this to your friend, not my client? Not Kristof – when you think about everything that they had been through together, do you really think Kristof did it?"

Avery gambled every once in a while. Usually in the casino. Rarely in the Courtroom, and almost never when someone's life and freedom were on the line. This was a gamble, but it was also what made him a great lawyer. He could read people very well.

"No, I… I was shocked when I learned he had been arrested for it as I never thought he would have done it."

"And that's all I am saying Ms Laurent… because it could have been someone else." Avery returned to his seat. "Thank you. No further questions."

The jury sat in heavy silence.

Turner was pissed. One of his star witnesses just flipped on him and helped the defence. He wanted to mitigate damage control but knew the witness had been turned, and even though he crafted a sound strategy, by bringing her on it backfired. His strategy was to move

forward with other experts.

CHAPTER 9 MOBILE EXTRACTION

TURNER ROSE ONCE more. "Your Honour, the Crown calls Forensic Analyst Raj Patel, specialist in mobile device extraction."

Raj Patel—used in many cases for the Crown regarding mobile phone forensic analysis, late thirties, precise, bespectacled—took the stand and confirmed the phone records: text from Kristof to Elle at 4:58 pm; several late-night texts from an unidentified number to Elle in the preceding months; no abusive messages from Kristof to anyone; communications with Sophie; but a narrative that very much corroborates the Prosecution's case. This was further corroborated by the mobile phone tower pings, showing that Elle's phone GPS was at her home for the entire evening, and that Kristof's phone was where he said he was – at the pub until around 11:15 pm, then making his way home and arriving home around 11:45 pm.

Turner closed with the familiar spin: "The final call. The unanswered questions. The rage that had been building. That fifteen-minute window of Mr Stanis being home after drinks, being emotionally agitated and hurt, to the point of stabbing his wife twenty-seven times before calling the police just after midnight." Turner used Patel to show that the pattern of communication between Elle and her former lover had significantly decreased – his second last witness; to bring the focus back to the hurt husband, who's motive to kill was from sheer jealousy and a crime of passion, and that his fingerprints were on the weapon, and that the death occurred during a window that he could have committed this crime.

Avery's cross was brief: he simply showed that the accuracy of the GPS is within 5-10m range, and that the mobile data actually tracked to be at the front of his house, rather than the inside of the house. Patel confirmed this, but it didn't help much. Avery attempted to plant seeds of doubt by stating Kristof could have been out the front before going the house, but this backfired with the response that his phone was 5-10m from the house, not necessarily Mr Stanis himself.

***

At 3:45 pm, Turner stood for the last time. "Your Honour, the Crown has one more witness to call. However, due to his line of work he is unable to attend until tomorrow morning. Might we adjourn until I can get this witness on the stand?"

A ripple of surprise moved through the gallery. Reporters exchanged quick glances; a few began typing furiously. Bluegum looked over his half-moon glasses at Turner, then at the clock.

"Very well, Mr Turner. The court will adjourn until tomorrow morning. Members of the jury, you are reminded of your obligations. Do not discuss the case, do not seek external information, and do not form any conclusions until all evidence is presented and you have heard my directions on the law."

"All rise."

The courtroom rose in a wave. Bluegum swept out. The jury filed away, some casting backward glances at the bar table as if trying to guess who the mystery witness might be. Kristof remained seated in the dock a moment longer, eyes on Avery—questioning, tense.

Avery leaned in. "He's saving Barker for last, I'd imagine. Wants the lead detective to tie it all up and leave the jury with that final image of certainty."

Kristof exhaled slowly. "Tomorrow , then."

"Depending on evidence-in-chief and then cross; Tomorrow or the day after, we start our side," Avery said firmly. "Alibi witnesses, character, documents. You stay quiet. We've got this."

The guards approached. Kristof gave a tight nod and was led away.

Avery gathered his notes, the courtroom emptying around him. Turner passed by the bar table on his way out, pausing just long enough for their eyes to meet. No words—just the faintest, professional nod of acknowledgment between opponents who knew the game was far from over.

***

As Avery left the courtroom, Ollie was already waiting, expression taut.

"Delaying for Barker," Ollie said quietly. "Classic. Lets the jury sleep on Patel's timeline gap and wake up to the cop who built the case."

Avery nodded. "It's strong. But it also gives us one more night to tighten our thread."

Ollie handed him the envelope. "Burner update came in late this afternoon. The *'we need to talk'* message on the night she died? Sent from a prepaid bought cash at a servo in Alexandria, two blocks from Greyrock's main site office." Ollie pointed out to some printed screenshots in the files, "CCTV is low-res—guy in a dark hoodie, face obscured—but the clerk remembers him paying exact change, no chit-chat. Time stamp fits the send window. The earlier two burners—*'Call me'* six weeks prior, *'Elle, this is serious…'* two weeks prior—

same purchase radius. All cash, all within walking distance of Greyrock's Alexandria hub."

Avery opened the rest of the envelope, scanned the printouts. The servo address stared back—too close for coincidence. "Greyrock again." Ollie continued. "I ran a deeper check on the director and senior staff. Nothing flashy—no criminal records, no obvious scandals. But one email popped: It's listed in internal Greyrock emails as coordinating with council assessors, but there's no other identifying information. No direct link to Elle yet, but whoever was receiving these emails was in the approvals loop. And get this: the only way I noticed it was by combing through those emails Elle received from Greyrock's requests and among the fifteen staff emails, all of them were *@greyrockcorp.com.au* except one which was *@greyrockcor.com.au*. Could it be a typo I thought? Possibly. But doing checks – the email actually exists. So the website itself has their filter general email as *admin@greyrockcorp.com.au* but nothing found for *admin@greyrockcor.com.au*"

"Interesting. And you're saying both of these emails were in all correspondence?"

"Yes, I haven't been able to find anything online. And our tech guy hasn't been able to link it to anything, other than letting me know that it exists on the server and it is still active and receiving emails. Oh and get this, this second email was only added in at the second request, aka after the first tender denial."

Avery folded the report. "Let's break this down again. Elle denies twice. Affair starts around the second denial. Email also included in that second denial onwards. Approval pushes through—forged signature. Affair ends. Then these sporadic burners pressure her. She dies before she can expose the forgery or irregularities. Greyrock gets its billion-dollar project. Someone inside—or connected—makes sure she can't talk."

Ollie's voice dropped. "Staged domestic. Used the real affair as cover. Framed the husband. Clean and simple."

Avery exhaled slowly. "Tomorrow Barker takes the stand. He'll try to close it tight—timeline, motive, no alternatives. We let him talk. Then we open defence with alibi. Danny Torres first—pub footage, timestamps, Kristof relaxed. Then character witnesses. After that, we tender the approvals, the signature mismatches, the burner purchase links. No direct accusation yet—just facts that scream alternative motive."

Ollie raised an eyebrow. "Judge and Prosecution's going to be furious when we start bringing Greyrock into open court, this late in the game."

Ollie was right. Avery had not brought up Greyrock at all. In fact, the only evidence so far are the fact that Elle worked in government in the building and development sector, but the Judge had previously ruled that work product remain confidential if it doesn't hold substantial weight and probative value to the case.

"I'll figure something out." Avery's tone was quiet steel. "Do I have anything that'll help me with cross tomorrow for Barker?"

"Nothing yet. He's clean or covered his tracks well for this case. It looks like everything proceeded to the timeline. Call came in, he and his partner were first detectives on scene early in the morning. The rest has already been covered and you've seen the interview tape."

Interview tape - that phrase had still stuck around, even though there was no interview tape anymore. Most of the time it was simply a video file either emailed and shared, or uploaded to a secure cloud that allowed those with "rights" to access.

They reached the street. The late-afternoon sun slanted across Phillip Street, casting long shadows. Ollie clapped him on the shoulder. "Get some rest. Tomorrow's the pivot."

Avery nodded. "See you at 9:30. Bring coffee."

Ollie grinned faintly. "Always."

"Oh and by the way, thanks for all this Ollie. You're saving the day."

"Don't mention it, boss."

Avery always thought it was funny that a "tough guy" like Ollie always became uncomfortable whenever he was praised for good work. Avery chuckled to himself and walked toward the Quay, the harbour breeze cutting through the day's tension. His phone buzzed—Rina: *Home early? Thai on the way. You sound like you need it xx*

He typed back: *On my way. Crown delayed closing for one more witness tomorrow. Barker. Need to decompress. I love you.*

Her reply: *Come tell me how you're going to turn it around I love you x*

He pocketed the phone and quickened his step.

CHAPTER 10 THE TIGHTROPE

RINA'S FLAT SMELLED of lemongrass, chili, and jasmine rice—takeaway containers open on the coffee table, two glasses of Shiraz waiting. She opened the door in an oversized T-shirt and yoga pants, hair loose, and pulled him inside. She kissed him—quick, grounding— then stepped back, studying his face.

"You look like the building sat on you."

"Turner delayed closing," Avery said, hanging his jacket.

"One more witness tomorrow morning. Barker. Lead detective. The one I was telling you about. He's saving the best for last—wants to end on the cop who built the case, hammer the timeline, the motive, the fifteen- minute window after the pub."

Rina handed him a glass. "And you?"

"Still figuring it out," Avery said. "Patel's evidence stung—the GPS ping at 11:45, right at the front of the house. Jury's going to chew on that fifteen-minutes all night. But Sophie flipped—said she never believed

Kristof capable. And the GPS is only 5–10 metres accurate. Phone could've been in his pocket out front while someone else was inside. Small crack, but it's there."

She sat beside him on the couch, legs tucked under her. "Detective Barker on the stand tomorrow… that's personal."

"Yes, but I have dealt with these types of cops before. They hate all defence lawyers. It shouldn't be new territory for me." Avery sighed, finally deciding to himself he wanted to stop thinking about the case and focus on spending time with Rina. "But for now, I actually want to give the case a break. I'm here with you."

"That's okay. I am open ears whenever you want to share with me. Just glad you're here to be honest. It's nice. Good news by the way…"

Avery looked up curiously.

"Yeah, the owner of this place gave her approval for you to move in today." Rina and Avery laughed at their inside joke.

"So, when this Barker's on the stand tomorrow? The Prosecution will use him to wrap up their case and point the finger at Kristof?" Rina changed the topic.

"He'll try." Avery met her eyes. "But the more he pushes back, the more the jury sees the cracks. If he gets defensive about why certain angles weren't investigated, it plants doubt right before we present our case."

Rina leaned closer, rested her forehead against his. "You're walking a tightrope."

"I know." He kissed her softly. "But I've got the balance."

They ate in quiet rhythm—pad see ew, spring rolls, shared glances. Between bites, she asked the question that had been sitting between them.

"If it's not Kristof, and you said you might know who's behind it… what happens when you start exposing that in open court?"

Avery set his fork down. "Well, it's dangerous game. Let's not worry about it tonight."

She traced a finger along his wrist. "Just promise me you'll watch your back."

"I promise." He turned her hand over, kissed her palm. "And when this is over, we're taking Luca to the beach. No phones, no files. Just us."

Her smile was small, real. "Deal."

Later, tangled in sheets that smelled of lemongrass and her shampoo, she traced lazy circles on his chest.

"You'll win this," she whispered.

He pulled her closer. "We'll win it."

Tomorrow Barker would take the stand.

But tonight belonged to them.

CHAPTER 11 Lead Investigator

THE ENERGY OF the courtroom morning felt charged, as if the overnight adjournment had only concentrated the tension rather than diffused it. The public gallery was packed to capacity—reporters squeezed shoulder-to-shoulder, legal observers from chambers, a few council colleagues who had quietly taken leave. The air held the faint scent of polished timber and stale coffee from the corridors, the low hum of air-conditioning underscoring every rustle of paper and creak of benches.

The jury filed in looking rested but watchful—notebooks open, pens poised, faces carrying the quiet residue of a night spent turning over Patel's fifteen-minute window, the GPS ping at 11:45 pm, and the unanswered question of who the mystery witness would be.

Kristof entered the dock between guards. He caught Avery's eye and gave a small, steady nod—no words needed. The strain was still etched deep, but the flicker of hope from yesterday had not gone out.

Once Justice Bluegum took the bench, the room settled.

"Mr Turner," Bluegum said, voice level, "the Crown may call its final witness."

Turner rose, composure intact, tie knotted with military precision.

"Your Honour, the Crown calls Detective Jacob Barker."

A murmur swept the gallery—reporters typing faster, a few heads turning. Barker entered from the side door, dark jacket over shirt and tie, jaw set, gaze sweeping the room before settling briefly on Avery. He took the oath with deliberate care, voice carrying the authority of twenty years on the job.

Turner began with the foundation.

"Detective Barker, you were the lead investigator on the death of Elle Stanis?"

"Yes. Attended the scene at approximately 4:15 am on 13 March last year, coordinated the investigation from that point forward."

Turner moved quickly to the arrest. "On the afternoon of 13 March, you arrested Kristof Stanis at his Marrickville residence. Did he make any spontaneous statements at that time?"

Barker nodded once. "As we placed him in the vehicle, he said, 'I didn't mean for any of this to happen.' He repeated it twice. 'I didn't mean for any of this.'"

The gallery inhaled. Several jurors leaned forward; one older man in the back row made a quick note.

Turner let the words settle. "Did he elaborate?"

"No. He went quiet after that. We cautioned him again and transported him to Marrickville Police Station."

Turner shifted to the overview. "Based on the totality of the evidence—the timeline, the forensics, the history of marital strain, the victim's final text to her friend about the accused 'asking again'—in your professional opinion as lead investigator, did this present as a domestic homicide driven by jealousy and unresolved anger?"

Barker's gaze was steady. "Yes. The evidence was consistent from the beginning. No forced entry. No sign of an intruder. The knife came from the victim's own kitchen drawer. The accused's prints were on the handle. The wounds—twenty-seven of them—were excessive, clustered around vital areas, indicative of rage. The kind of rage that builds over months of betrayal and unanswered questions. The neighbour heard raised voices around 10:45 pm The accused's phone pinged at the front of the house around 11:45 pm Fifteen minutes is more than enough time for a man who'd been drinking, who'd been carrying hurt for months, to lose control."

Turner paused, letting the jury absorb the weight. "And the absence of high-velocity spatter on his clothing?"

"Consistent with him changing or cleaning up before calling triple zero. He had time. He knew the house. He knew how to avoid leaving obvious traces."

Turner finished quietly. "Thank you, Detective."

Avery rose without haste. He walked to the lectern slowly, letting the silence pull the jury's attention. Barker's stare was hard, almost expectant—daring him to push.

"Detective Barker," Avery began, voice calm and even, "you described Mr Stanis saying 'I didn't mean for any of this to happen' during the arrest. Did he say those words after you informed him his wife had been found deceased?"

"Yes," Barker said. "We told him at the scene that she was dead, as we confirm with all subjects. But we also do this to gauge reactions as part of our investigation."

"So, he was reacting to the news of her death—not confessing to causing it?"

"That's one way to interpret it."

"Is there another?"

Barker's jaw tightened fractionally. "He could have been expressing regret for what he'd done."

Avery nodded mildly. "Could have. But he didn't say 'I killed her.' He didn't say 'I stabbed her.' He said he didn't mean for any of this to happen. Correct?"

"Correct."

Avery shifted to the timeline. "You placed great weight on the neighbour's report of raised voices around 10:45 pm the night before, to create a theme of an unhappy marriage. But the medical evidence gives a window of 10:30 pm to midnight, and Mr Stanis has witnesses and CCTV placing him at the Royal Hotel until 11:15 pm. It would seem that not being physically present, should outweigh the notion of an unhappy marriage theory-"

"I object, Your Honour – he's testifying for the witness." Turner rose and cutoff Avery.

"Mr Santos." Bluegum simply said, without further explanation.

Avery nodded back to the judge, then continue.

"Detective, did you investigate or confirm with the witnesses who placed Mr Stanis at the pub that night?"

"Yes. They confirmed he was there."

"And the footage?"

"Showed him leaving at 11:15."

"So, it is possible—given the medical window—that the attack occurred before he left the pub and prior to him arriving home?"

Barker paused, eyes narrowing. "The neighbour heard raised voices at 10:45 previously. The overall picture—"

"Possible," Avery repeated, cutting in cleanly. "The medical window starts at 10:30 pm, and Mr Stanis was still at the pub until 11:15, confirmed by multiple witnesses and time-stamped CCTV. You accept that?"

Barker's voice was flat. "The footage shows him there until 11:15. But the neighbour's evidence with the prior arguments, his fingerprints on the knife and blood on some clothing, all aligns that regardless of what the window was – he was the killer."

Avery paused, letting it sit. "And in your investigation, did you explore any alternative suspects? Anyone who might have had reason to harm Elle Stanis?"

Barker's expression hardened. "We followed the evidence. It led to the accused."

"Did you investigate irregularities in her work at the council? The development approvals she handled?"

"We looked at her life. No threats from work. No enemies."

Avery paused, voice still level. "Detective, you've described this as a classic domestic homicide. But isn't it true that in cases where a victim is silenced to prevent exposure—of corruption, improper influence, financial gain—the scene is often staged to look domestic? Overkill wounds. A kitchen knife left behind. A husband with a plausible but painful motive placed at the scene?"

Turner rose instantly. "Objection—speculative, argumentative, no foundation."

"Objection allowed," Bluegum said promptly. "Mr Santos, confine yourself to questions."

Avery accepted the ruling with a small nod. "Detective, did your investigation rule out the possibility that someone else staged this to look like a crime of passion?"

Barker's voice was flat, controlled. "We found no evidence of staging. The evidence pointed to the accused."

"Thank you. No further questions, Your Honour, but we reserve the right to recall this witness at a later time." Avery returned to his seat.

Kristof leaned in, voice barely audible. "He's lying through his teeth. I did not confess to killing her, that's not what I meant."

"Be quiet." Avery murmured back, "He's protecting something. And the jury just heard him dodge on the early window." Then Avery turned to Kristof with a serious look, "And do not show any anger in front of the jury. You understand me?"

Bluegum glanced at Turner. "Re-examination?"

Turner rose briefly. "No re-examination, Your Honour." He then looked down at his folder, then back up to the judge. "If Your Honour pleases, that concludes evidence for the Prosecution."

Bluegum addressed the court. "The Crown closes its case."

The room exhaled. Murmurs rose as people shifted.

Bluegum turned to the jury. "Members of the jury, the Crown has now concluded the presentation of its evidence. The defence will now have the opportunity to present its case. Mr Santos, you may open."

<u>CHAPTER 12</u> OPENING

AVERY ROSE AGAIN. He buttoned his jacket once, walked to the centre of the bar table—no lectern, no visible notes. He faced the jury directly, voice low enough that they had to lean in.

"Ladies and gentlemen," he began, "the Crown has told you a powerful story. A husband betrayed. A wife unfaithful. Pain that built until it exploded in twenty-seven stab wounds. Rage. Jealousy. A crime of passion. It is a story that explains the horror neatly—except the facts that refuse to fit."

He paused, letting the silence do its work.

"Mr Kristof Stanis did not confess. Not to police. Not in custody. Not anywhere. The Crown relies on overheard sobs through a prison wall from a man chasing parole—vague words, no details, no admission of violence. The fingerprints on the knife? Consistent with someone picking it up in shock, finding his wife dying. The blood spatter on his clothes? Minimal. Not the pattern you expect from a man who inflicted twenty-seven wounds at close range."

Avery took a single step closer.

"The Crown says the time of death aligns with the narrative they are trying to produce; an argument the night before, Mr Stanis own fingerprints on the knife and his wife's blood on his clothes – ignoring the fact that he was the one who called for help in the first place. What doesn't fit in their narrative though, is what they are not saying. The medical evidence gives a window: 10:30 pm to midnight. Mr Stanis was at the Royal Hotel in Newtown with three workmates—laughing, buying rounds, relaxed—until 11:15 pm There is CCTV footage. There are witnesses. The pathologist could not exclude death occurring during the time Mr Stanis was still at the pub. The Crown must prove beyond reasonable doubt that he was not there."

He let that land.

"And motive? Yes, there was hurt. An affair. Questions that lingered. But Mr Stanis forgave. They went to counselling. They planned family time. They were rebuilding. The Crown asks you to see a man who could not let go. We will ask you to see something else: a timeline too perfect to be coincidence. A woman who denied a major development application twice. Then, suddenly, it is approved—over what appears to be her forged signature. Four weeks later she is dead. Someone had motive far stronger than jealousy. Someone stood to lose millions if not billions, if Elle Stanis spoke up about what she knew. Irregularities. Improper influence. Silence bought with blood, then dressed up to look like a domestic tragedy."

Avery's voice remained calm, almost gentle.

"This is not about tricks or technicalities. It should about reasonable doubt. In actual fact, it is a about the truth. Because the truth is my client did not do this, but there is a guilty party out there who is responsible for the tragic death of Elle Stanis. And that's where the guilt lies. With them. What we will prove to you in our case is that not only is my client innocent of these charges, but we will also shine the light on the guilty party by bringing them out of the shadows, which they hide. When you have seen the footage, heard the witnesses, examined the documents, you will see that doubt for my client is not only reasonable. It is overwhelming. And guilt for someone else–well that's undeniable."

He gave a small nod. "Thank you."

He returned to his seat. Kristof exhaled slowly beside him.

Bluegum addressed the jury. "The defence has now opened its case. Mr Santos, you may call your first witness."

Avery rose. "The defence calls Mr Daniel 'Danny' Torres."

Danny Torres entered—late thirties, broad-shouldered, still carrying the faint scent of site dust despite a fresh shirt. He took the oath with straightforward confidence.

Avery began easily.

"Mr Torres, how long have you known Kristof Stanis?"

"Eight years. Worked together on big builds. He's solid. Reliable. The bloke you want on your crew."

"On the evening of 12 March last year, were you with him?"

"Yeah. Knocked off around 5:30. The four of us headed to the Royal in Newtown. End-of-week ritual."

Avery tendered the CCTV stills—time-stamped: Kristof at the bar at 10:48 pm, laughing; 11:12 pm, coat on, heading out.

"These images show Mr Stanis in the pub at those times?"

"That's him. That's us."

"Did he leave early?"

"No chance. We walked out together at 11:15."

Avery paused. "In all the years you've known him, has Mr Stanis ever shown a violent temper?"

Danny shook his head. "Never. He's the one who breaks up arguments on site."

Avery concluded the witness by presenting Kristof's side as a well-mannered down-to-earth regular guy. Someone the jury can all sympathize with and even relate to.

Turner's cross was tight but couldn't move the timestamps or demeanour.

Bluegum adjourned for lunch. The jury left looking more thoughtful than they had in days.

***

In the corridor, Ollie waited with coffee.

"Footage landed clean," Ollie said. "Jury's staring at those clocks."

Avery took the cup. "Good. Barker's testimony gave us the opening. Now we build."

Kristof was escorted past. He caught Avery's eye.

Avery gave a firm nod. "We're moving, mate. Bit by bit."

The afternoon session reconvened at 2:15 pm Courtroom 11 had grown warmer, the air thick with the scent of polished timber and the low buzz of anticipation. The jury returned looking more engaged—notebooks ready, eyes flicking to the bar table as Avery rose.

"Your Honour, the defence calls Mr Jason 'Jase' Kelly."

Jase Kelly entered—early forties, lean, still in work boots polished for court. Another site mate from the Marrickville project. He took the oath with easy confidence.

Avery led him through the same ground: arrival at the Royal just after 6:00 pm, rounds, laughter, Kristof relaxed and joking the whole night, departure together at 11:15 pm

Avery tendered more CCTV stills—Kristof raising a glass at 10:55 pm, arm around Jase's shoulder; 11:10 pm, coat on, heading for the door.

"These images show Mr Stanis in the pub during the critical window?"

"Yeah. That's him. That's us."

"Did he show any signs of agitation? Anger? Checking his phone obsessively?"

Jase shook his head. "None. He was the same bloke he always is—quick with a joke, buying rounds, talking footy and the kids. No edge. No mood swings."

Turner's cross was brisk—highlighting the friendship, the drinks consumed—but the timestamps and demeanour held firm.

Next came the pub manager, a short, brisk woman in her fifties who confirmed the group's regular custom, the CCTV system's reliability, and the 11:15 pm closing for them.

By 3:45 pm, Bluegum adjourned for the day.

"Members of the jury, we will resume tomorrow at 10:00 am The usual reminders apply."

"All rise."

As the jury left, Avery caught a few of them glancing toward the defence table—not with hostility, but with something closer to curiosity.

In the corridor, Ollie was waiting again.

"Two more alibi bricks down," Ollie said. "Jury's starting to do the maths. If death was between 10:30 and 11:00, Kristof was still at the pub. Barker couldn't close that gap."

Avery nodded. "Good. Tomorrow, we shift gears. Character witnesses in the morning—foreman mate, kids' teacher—then we tender the approvals. The mismatched signatures first. If Bluegum lets them in, the jury sees the timeline overlap: denials, affair start, approval push, affair end, death. They'll start asking who benefited."

Ollie handed him a fresh printout. "Handwriting prelim just arrived. Expert's confident—the third signature shows pressure differences, loop variations, baseline drift. Not hers."

Avery folded it into his briefcase. "Good. We will use that this week." Avery walked out into the late-afternoon light on Phillip Street. The harbour breeze cut through the day's tension. His phone buzzed—Rina: *I've got dinner on. You sounded strong today xx*

He typed back: *Excited to see you*

Her reply: *Me too xx*

The day had gone as Avery had planned. Trials are similar to war; the more battles won, the easier it is for total victory. But there were plenty of battles ahead, and Avery was anticipating.

He pocketed the phone and headed for the Quay.

The Crown had closed.

The defence had begun.

And the jury was listening.

The contest continued.

CHAPTER 13 THE ALIBI

THE NEXT MORNING light in Courtroom 11 was crisp and unforgiving, the kind that made every shadow look sharper. The public gallery had grown even fuller—word had spread overnight that the defence was now presenting its case, and the first day of alibi evidence had drawn curious observers from the legal precinct. Reporters typed steadily, the soft clack of keyboards a constant undercurrent.

The jury filed in, notebooks ready, expressions more attentive than they had been in weeks. Whatever doubts Barker's testimony had planted, the alibi witnesses yesterday had given them something solid to chew on.

Kristof settled in the dock, shoulders a little less rounded than before. He caught Avery's eye and gave a small nod—quiet trust.

"All rise."

"Mr Santos," Bluegum said, "the defence may continue."

More character witnesses similar to Jase Kelly and Daniel Torres were presented. Brick by brick, Avery thought to himself, until the final character witness of the morning session: Sarah Thompson, the primary school teacher for Kristof's daughter. Mid-thirties, calm, composed.

Avery led her gently.

"Ms Thompson, how long have you known Kristof Stanis?"

"Four years. His daughter's in my class. He's at almost every parent-teacher meeting, every school event. Always on time, always engaged."

"In your interactions with him, has he ever shown anger or aggression?"

"Never. He's patient. Kind. When his daughter had a rough patch last year, he worked with me every step — homework plans, reading support. The kids love him. He's the dad who volunteers for reading days."

Turner had no cross. The point was made.

By 12:30 pm, Bluegum adjourned for lunch. The jury left looking more settled—character evidence had softened the image of Kristof from "jealous husband" to "steady family man."

In the corridor Ollie waited with coffee and a slim folder.

"Character landed soft," Ollie said. "Jury's starting to see the man, not the motive."

Avery took the coffee. "Good. Afternoon: we tender the approvals. First two denials in Elle's name, third with the mismatched signature. If Bluegum allows it, the jury sees the timeline overlap. Then the burner purchases near Greyrock's office."

Ollie handed him the folder. "Handwriting report finalised. Expert's conclusion: high confidence the third signature is not Elle's. Pressure inconsistencies, loop formation variations, baseline drift—all indicators of tracing or simulation. We are lucky she's working in the city today – she said she can testify if you cover all expenses again."

Avery scanned it. "Perfect. We lead with this after lunch. Her expenses include her urgency fee?"

Ollie nodded, knowing that her urgency fee meant an extra couple of thousand dollars she was charging.

"Okay, we need her in. Do it." Avery accepted.

Kristof was escorted past. He caught Avery's eye.

"Thanks for today, I owe those guys some more beers if I'm ever outta here. And Ms Thompson too–I didn't realise she paid attention so much to all the parents. Glad she was here on my side. She loved Elle too." Kristof asked quietly.

Avery nodded. "Now it's our turn to tell the story. But you don't need to worry about that, just get some rest tonight. Hang in there."

Kristof exhaled, "I will."

Avery watched him go, the guards' footsteps fading down the corridor. He stood for a moment, the folder from Ollie heavy in his hand. The handwriting report was solid—high confidence, clear indicators of forgery. It would be tendered, and the jury would see the timeline overlap in black and white: denials, affair start, forged approval, affair end, death. But something still didn't sit right with Avery—he believed Kristof was upset about losing Elle, but there was something more, something that tugged at Avery making him believe maybe Kristof wasn't innocent of everything. Avery believed him. He had to. Yet that flicker of something guarded in his client's eyes kept surfacing, small but persistent, like a note played just off-key. He filed it away, same as before.

He shook it off and headed for the lifts. There was no time for doubt now. The defence case was rolling.

***

The afternoon session resumed at 2:15 pm The courtroom had grown warmer, the air thick with the scent of polished timber and the low buzz of anticipation. The jury returned looking more attentive— notebooks open, eyes flicking to the bar table as Avery rose.

"Your Honour, the defence calls Dr. Elizabeth Morrow, forensic document examiner."

Dr. Morrow entered—late fifties, sharp-eyed, white blouse under a navy blazer. She took the oath with quiet authority and sat.

Avery began with credentials: twenty-five years specialising in handwriting and document authenticity, hundreds of court appearances, published papers on forgery indicators.

"Dr. Morrow, did you examine three council development approval documents tendered in this matter?"

"Yes. The first two denials and the third approval, all bearing signatures purporting to be Elle Stanis's."

Avery tendered the documents. "Can you describe your findings?"

Dr. Morrow gestured to the projected images. "The first two signatures are consistent in pressure, stroke formation, loop structure, and baseline alignment—all hallmarks of natural writing. The third signature shows significant deviations: inconsistent pen pressure, irregular loop formation, baseline drift, and tremor-like hesitations. These are classic indicators of tracing, simulation, or guided forgery. In my opinion, to a high degree of confidence, the third signature is not that of Elle Stanis."

Turner rose. "Objection—relevance. These documents relate to council work, not the murder. No foundation linking forgery to the offence."

Bluegum looked at Avery. "Mr Santos?"

"Your Honour, the documents go directly to motive. The third approval was fast-tracked after two denials by the deceased. The timing overlaps precisely with the start and end of the affair the Crown relies on for motive. If the approval was obtained by forgery, someone had a powerful financial incentive to silence Ms Stanis before she could expose it. This creates a reasonable alternative explanation for the killing—far stronger than jealousy—and therefore reasonable doubt."

Turner countered. "This is speculative. No evidence connects any third party to the scene. It's a fishing expedition."

Bluegum considered for a moment. "The evidence is admitted for the limited purpose of assessing whether there is a reasonable possibility of an alternative motive. The jury will be directed accordingly. Proceed, Mr Santos."

Avery continued. "Dr. Morrow, the timeline: first denial eight months beforehand, second denial two months beforehand, third approval four weeks before death. Does that affect your opinion?"

"It does not change the forensic conclusion. But the sudden approval after consistent denials is unusual in my experience with public records, though I am not working directly in the sector so my knowledge is limited."

Turner's cross was sharp but narrow—challenging the degree of confidence, suggesting natural variation. He landed a blow though on that point regarding Dr.

Morrow's experience with public records and building and development work. It was 50/50 with the jury for now. But regarding the main sticking point Avery was using to paint his picture–Dr. Morrow held firm: "Variation within one signature is normal. These differences are between documents. They are not natural."

Bluegum gave the limiting direction to the jury: "This evidence is admitted solely to assist you in determining whether there is a reasonable possibility of another motive for the killing. It is not evidence that any particular person committed the offence, nor that forgery occurred for any specific reason. You must consider it only in that context."

The jury listened intently. A few made notes; one woman in the front row glanced at Kristof, then back at the projected signatures.

By 4:00 pm, Bluegum adjourned until morning.

"Members of the jury, we resume tomorrow at 10:00 am The usual reminders apply."

As the courtroom emptied, Avery caught a few jurors lingering on the bar table—thoughtful, not dismissive. The forged signature had landed. However, Avery was worried that he could still lose the jury's interest. He knew that juries love eating up conspiracy theories, but the truth is, right now, all Avery had was a bunch of theories and ideas that misdirect the jury. The Prosecution still had a stronger case.

In the corridor Ollie was waiting. He likes this spot as it allows him to stay close to the Court should he receive instruction to return, or to leave for some other task.

"Handwriting hit hard," Ollie said quietly. "Jury's looking at those signatures like they're seeing them for the first time."

Avery nodded. "Bluegum let it in. Limited, but they heard the words: not hers. Tomorrow, we tender the burner purchases near Greyrock's office. The jury starts connecting dots."

Ollie handed him an updated report. "Servo clerk statement just came in. Guy in hoodie bought the '*we need to talk'* burner with exact change. Two blocks from Greyrock Alexandria site. Same pattern for the earlier burners."

Avery folded it away. "Good. Have you been able to ID him yet?"

"Still working on it. I'll let you know if we get something. We are trying multiple angles, and even external cameras to get another view."

Avery walked out into the late-afternoon light on Phillip Street. The harbour breeze cut through the tension. His phone buzzed—Rina: *Home? Dinner's ready. You were brilliant today xx*

Avery thought it was nice that Rina was in the courtroom again today for a some of the questioning. He noticed she had been visiting for an hour or two, and it felt to him that she would always coincidentally show up at a time of need to give him that extra strength.

He thought about the day more.

The alibi was solid.

Character was in place.

The forged signature was on record.

Tomorrow the other motive would start to breathe.

CHAPTER 14 DOCUMENT EXAMINATION

THE COURTROOM AT 10:00 am felt different today—sharper, more expectant, as though the air itself had thickened with the weight of what was coming. The public gallery was full to capacity, but quieter than usual. Reporters sat with laptops half-closed, fingers hovering, watching rather than typing. A few legal observers from Phillip Street had slipped in, drawn by word that the defence was moving beyond alibi into something more dangerous. The jury filed in looking more alert than they had in days—notebooks open, some already scanning the bar table where Avery's new exhibits waited like loaded weapons.

Kristof entered the dock between guards. He gave Avery the small nod that had become their ritual—quiet trust. But today Avery noticed something else: the way Kristof's gaze drifted briefly toward the gallery, then snapped back forward, as if daydreaming afar then falling back into reality again. It could be nothing, after all he was on trial for the murder of his wife *–don't worry about it*, Avery thought to himself.

The usual ritual continued.

"Mr Santos," Bluegum said, "the defence may continue."

Avery rose. "Your Honour, the defence recalls Mr Rajesh Patel for further cross-examination on supplementary material obtained since his original testimony."

Turner was on his feet before Avery finished the sentence. "Objection—relevance, prejudice, and procedural unfairness. The Crown has closed its case. This is new evidence masquerading as recall."

Bluegum looked at Avery over his glasses. "Mr Santos?"

Avery kept his voice even. "Your Honour, Mr Patel was the Crown's own phone forensics analyst. The supplementary data comes from the same extraction process already in evidence—additional detail on three untraceable messages and their purchase locations. This material was not fully pursued in the Crown case and goes directly to the alternative motive opened in cross-examination of Detective Barker and foreshadowed in the defence opening. It is limited rebuttal, highly probative of reasonable doubt, and in the interests of justice."

Turner: "This is ambush. No foundation linking these burners to any offence or person. It invites speculation."

Bluegum considered for a long moment, eyes moving between counsel. "The witness is the Crown's expert. The material relates to records already admitted. Leave is granted for limited recall, confined strictly to the new data. The jury will be directed on its use. Proceed, Mr Santos."

Rajesh Patel returned to the stand—same measured calm, same bespectacled precision. He took the oath again without flourish.

Avery began. "Mr Patel, since your original evidence for the Crown, have you reviewed additional data from the same phone extraction?"

"Yes. Supplementary report dated yesterday."

Avery tendered the report and projected the first page: three message screenshots, timestamps clear. "These are three untraceable messages received by Elle Stanis in the weeks before her death: '*Call me*' six weeks prior, '*Elle, this is serious, I am sorry but let me explain*' two weeks prior, and '*we need to talk*' on the night of 12 March, the same night she was murdered. Confirm these were not from the accused's number or any known contact?"

"Correct. All three from different prepaid numbers, no history with the victim's known contacts."

Avery advanced the slide to the map overlay. "And the purchase locations of these burners?"

"Purchased with cash at three separate locations—a convenience store in Alexandria, a service station on Bourke Road, and another store on Gardeners Road."

"How were you able to obtain that these were the locations of the burners linked to these phone numbers?"

"Well, it's actually not that difficult if you know what you are looking for. We ran the IMEIs through the manufacturer's distribution logs. That led us to a bulk shipment sent to the retail outlets in those postcodes. From there, it was just a matter of matching the activation timestamps with the store's point-of-sale records and CCTV. Not to mention, in Australia it's legally required that a purchaser of a phone provide an ID in order to have that sim activated."

"Were you able to identify that ID?"

"No, that's not my job. My job is simple forensic analysis specialising in telecommunication hardware and devices."

"It sounds like you did a lot of extra work here, which wasn't necessarily done at first. Can you tell us why?"

There was a momentary pause, whilst the jury eagerly waited.

"No, there's no particular reason. Some things just take time to be received, particularly when it comes to telco providers, and I have a duty to ensure that all my evidence and testimony I provide is factually accurate and correct."

There was actually a discovery that benefited Avery in the week leading to this moment, whilst being detrimental to Patel and the Crown. Ollie was able to find all this without Patel—he had traced the IMEIs back to the stores. He was unable to identify the buyer of the burners, but he was able to secure all the CCTV footage matching the purchase. However, Ollie, or Avery for that matter, could not use what he had found. Not yet, at least. Thankfully, Ollie had also uncovered something about Patel's past. Now, someone reminded Patel that if he were to make a mistake again, it would have serious consequences on his career. It wasn't Avery, or Ollie for that matter… however, Avery and Ollie do know a lot of people from a lot of places. The key was to ensure that it wouldn't link back to Avery or his client. For moments like this, people usually have particular pressure points. For Patel, it was the threat of being exposed by a reporter doing their due diligence on everyone involved in the case. And because it is a news reporter, it doesn't matter if there's any bias for or against either side of an ongoing case, because everyone knows that people pay attention to the drama more than the details. That's what was lingering of Patel's head. That's why Patel had been nudged and more than willing to retake the stand.

"Well, thank you for being so diligent, Mr Patel." Avery continued. "Now, did you know that these three are all within a 1.5 km radius of the Greyrock Developments site office in Alexandria."

"Objection! Relevance?" Turner was visibly annoyed with the look of *where is this going* on his face.

A low murmur moved through the gallery.

"Mr Santos?"

"Your Honour, this will be highly relevant, if the Court will just indulge me for one moment."

"You may proceed, but I am putting on the record that I can reverse any findings with the jury should this turn into a fishing expedition or stray too far from this hearing."

"Thank you, Your Honour." Avery resumed. "Now Mr Patel, as I was stating, were you aware that all three of these prepaid locations were within that short radius of Greyrock?" Avery at the same time put up on the digital whiteboard a map showing the locations and the radius from Greyrock headquarters.

Several jurors leaned forward; one woman in the front row made a note, then glanced at her neighbour as if to confirm what she'd just seen. The older man in the back row tapped his pen once, twice, eyes fixed on the red circle Avery had highlighted on the map.

Avery paused, letting the image sit. "Mr Patel, in your professional opinion as a mobile forensics specialist, is this degree of geographic clustering statistically unusual for three unrelated prepaid purchases?"

Patel considered. "Not necessarily. Three random purchases of prepaid sim cards and phones from three stores are completely expected."

"That makes sense. But then when you consider the fact that each of those separate sims and burners, all texted the same phone number, in this case, the victim's number all within two months apart leading up to her death – what do you make of the probability and those findings then?"

"I object, Your Honour, the question is outside the expertise of the witness."

"Your Honour, this is the Crown's own mobile forensic analyst, and when the Crown introduced this witness, they spent almost fifteen minutes detailing Mr Patel's expertise, history and experience working on cases alongside the Prosecution. I am asking Mr Patel due to his credentials and expertise, as already presented to the Court by the Crown earlier.

"Objection overruled. I'll allow the witness to answer."

"Well, I guess in that scenario, the probability of three independent cash purchases that all end up randomly texting the same corresponding phone number, clustering so tightly around one commercial site is very very low—well below what would be expected by chance."

"So, based on your experience, what does the geographical location have to do with that cluster?"

"Well, if it was all the same buyer, then my experience would tell me that he would either live or work in that vicinity."

"Nothing further." Avery concluded.

Turner rose for cross. "Mr Patel, these numbers are untraceable. No direct link to Greyrock Developments or any specific individual known to the Court, correct?"

"Correct."

"No evidence anyone from Greyrock purchased them?"

"No direct evidence."

"And is there any evidence that there the phones were bought by the same man or woman?"

"No."

"And the defence have made it clear you have a vast amount of experience in Courtrooms, testifying to your expert opinions, so based on that experience–have you ever had a case where the defence would attempt to distract the jury by pointing to multiple different opinions and ideas?"

"I object. Your Honour!?"

"Apologies, Your Honour. Question withdrawn. Nothing further." Turner jabbed back. It was a good response.

Turner sat. He had scored a small point—but the points scored by Avery were greater. The jury had seen the circle already. Turner on the other hand, had taken this point down for his closing argument – another defence tactic of smoke and mirrors, by pointing to something completely unrelated like Greyrock, just to distract the jury…

Bluegum gave the limiting direction: "Members of the jury, this evidence is admitted solely to assist you in assessing whether there is a reasonable possibility of another motive or explanation for the killing. It is not evidence that any particular person sent these messages or committed the offence. You must consider it only in that context."

The jury absorbed it in near-silence. A few exchanged glances; the woman in the front row looked back at the projected map one more time before closing her notebook.

***

Avery had one final witness before lunch: a council records clerk who authenticated the three approval documents as official records. Turner offered no cross—saving his fire for closings.

Bluegum adjourned at 12:45 pm this time. One of the jury members had to leave early for a family emergency.

"Members of the jury, we resume tomorrow at 10:00 am The usual reminders apply."

As the courtroom emptied, Avery lingered at the bar table, watching the jury file out. A few looked back—not at him, but at the screen where the map still glowed, the red circle tight around Greyrock's office. One juror, the older man with the pen, paused in the doorway, eyes narrowing as if working something out.

In the corridor Ollie was waiting, two flat whites in hand.

"Burner circle landed," Ollie said quietly. "I saw the front-row woman stare at that map like she'd just seen a ghost. They're starting to do the geography."

Avery took the coffee. "Bluegum kept it limited, but they heard the radius. Tomorrow, we tender the email domain anomaly and the project manager bonus timing. The jury asks who added that second address—and why only after the second denial."

Ollie handed him a slim update. "Tech confirmed: *@greyrockcor.com.au* domain is active, no public footprint. It only appears in Elle's incoming correspondence after the second denial. Someone added it quietly, then used it for coordination."

Avery folded it away. "Good. We'll continue to build on that, now it's our turn."

He stepped outside into the midday sun on Phillip Street. The harbour glittered in the distance, sharp and indifferent. For the first time in weeks, Avery felt the case tilting—not just toward doubt, but toward something concrete. He hoped his hunch was right. He knew this was an important time to prove it, the jury was no longer just listening, they were beginning to question, and he had promised them to show them the light.

He pulled out his phone and texted Rina: *Burners in. Jury's connecting dots but they're done for the day. Coming home for lunch. Need a minute to breathe.*

Her reply came fast: *Door's open. I've got you. Hurry xx*

He smiled—small, real—and started walking. The weight was still there, but for the first time, it felt like it might lift.

CHAPTER 15 THE GREYROCK CIRCLE

THE MORNING AFTER the burner evidence, the air in the Phillip Street corridor felt like it was holding its breath. Avery arrived early, his mind playing back the way the jury had stared at the map of Alexandria. The "Greyrock circle" was no longer just a theory; it was a physical mark on the case, a stain of doubt that the Crown's pristine narrative of a jealous husband couldn't quite scrub away.

Ollie was already there, leaning against a marble pillar with a folder that looked thicker than yesterday's. He didn't offer a greeting, just handed over a flat white and tapped the top of the file with a heavy thumb.

"I stayed up with the tech guy threading that *@greyrockcor.com.au* anomaly," Ollie said, his voice a low rumble that barely carried past the two of them. "It's not just a ghost domain. We found the metadata on the internal server for the project's internal structure and timeline and other emails which weren't secured"

Avery flipped the folder open, scanning the dense spreadsheets. "And?"

"The Marrickville project needed to be finalised by April. There is a project report timeline dating checkpoints, but there were also a couple of other emails between employees at Greyrock discussing if they'll meet the April deadline. Now I know it's nothing concrete, but you put it together then you'll see–"

"–the project needed to be approved by April in order to proceed. Elle was blocking it, so they did something to get rid of that roadblock." Avery finished Ollie's sentence.

"Exactly. We couldn't find out who the second email domain was linked to though. It's a dead end. Anyone who has the email and password can log into it and check their emails from anywhere and mostly any device."

Avery stared at the dates. The financial motive wasn't just large; it was urgent. He had read in the news that the Marrickville project was at least a $1.3 billion dollar development. It was a ticking clock. "Let's go back to Elle, so if she denies it a third time, the window closes."

"Exactly," Ollie nodded. "And there's more. I thought that the forged document is one thing, but it would still need to be approved in the next tier. These government systems usually have a filtration process to stop these things from happening. So, the 'final' version of the forged document that was sent to the archives. It bypassed the department's main server. Someone had help from the inside, or they knew exactly how to ghost the system. One day, the file was labelled as pending within the system, and then all of a sudden it was approved and finalised."

Avery closed the folder with a sharp snap. "We'll need to tender this through a rebuttal expert or a subpoenaed records clerk. Turner will fight it, but Bluegum is already letting the motive in."

"One more thing," Ollie added, his eyes shifting toward the elevators, his expression hardening. "Barker was at the Rocks last night. Not at the Anchor, but he was parked a block away from Rina's when I left. He's not just rattled anymore. He's stalking the perimeter."

The coffee suddenly tasted like battery acid. Avery didn't answer. He turned and walked into Courtroom 11, the weight of the folder in his hand feeling like a live wire.

***

The morning session was technical and gruelling—a rebuttal pathologist Avery had called to challenge the "rage" narrative that Dr. Hale had so meticulously constructed.

"Dr. Aris, you've reviewed the spatter patterns and the wound clustering?" Avery asked, standing at the lectern, his voice echoing in the hushed chamber.

"I have," the doctor replied, adjusting his glasses. "While the number of wounds is high, the lack of high-velocity spatter on the accused's upper body is significant. In a truly frenzied attack involving twenty-seven thrusts, the lack of blowback on the perpetrator—

the absence of arterial misting on the face and chest—is highly improbable."

"And the staging?" Avery pressed, glancing at the jury.

"The placement of the knife—perfectly aligned with the victim's reach but covered in the accused's prints—can be interpreted as a simulated domestic scene," the doctor stated clinically. "We have seen these before in our internal testing simulations to chart and track blood-splatter to predict real life scenarios."

Turner's cross-examination was a surgical attempt to discredit the "staging" theory, but the damage was done. The jury was looking at the dock not with horror, but with a growing, analytical doubt. They were no longer seeing a monster; they were seeing a man who might have been a convenient prop in someone else's play.

When the court adjourned for the evening, Avery waited until the gallery cleared before heading for the lifts. He found Detective Barker waiting in the stairwell alcove, his posture aggressive, an unlit cigarette tucked behind his ear.

"You think you're smart, Santos," Barker spat, stepping into Avery's path, his voice low enough not to carry far but sharp enough to cut. "Dragging Greyrock into this. You'll do anything to defend scum and killers. Typical defence lawyers – will spin any story to hide the real one. Elle was a beautiful loving woman who did not deserve this! She was too good for Kristof"

"I understand a forged signature and a billion-dollar project, Detective," Avery said, his voice cold and even. "Why didn't you? Or did you just prefer the easy story?"

Barker stepped closer, his face inches from Avery's, the scent of stale tobacco and desperation clinging to him. "The 'easy story' is the one where a husband kills his cheating wife. It happens every day. What doesn't happen is a lawyer like you walking away clean after trying to burn down a major development for a wife-killer."

"Is that a threat?"

"It's a forecast," Barker growled. "Drop the Greyrock angle. You don't want to drag their name through the mud, especially to get some killer off. If you keep digging into the council approvals, you won't just lose the case. You'll lose everything."

Barker turned sharply and disappeared down the stairs, the door clattering shut with a metallic finality.

Avery stood in the silence of the stairwell for a long minute. His hand went to his pocket, feeling the vibration of his phone.

Rina: *Home yet? Luca is asleep. I'm worried about you x.*

Avery didn't reply immediately. He thought about the *@greyrockcor* email, the forged signature, and the way Kristof had looked at the gallery earlier that day. Barker's tone changed. He was no longer hating the fact that Avery was a defence lawyer, but his focus had shifted to scaring Avery away from Greyrock. Avery knew there was something more to this.

He walked out toward Phillip Street, the Sydney skyline glowing with a cold, corporate light. He spotted

Ollie waiting by his car, his face illuminated by the blue light of his phone.

"Avery," Ollie said, looking up with a strange, taut intensity. "I just got a hit on a secondary server. I found something. Something Barker definitely didn't want us to find."

"What is it?" Avery asked, his pulse quickening.

Ollie shook his head, glancing around the darkening street. "Not here. It's deep, and it changes everything. Let's get to the Anchor. I'll walk you through it tonight. You're going to need this for Barker's recall tomorrow."

Avery nodded, the weight of the new secret settling over him. He was mentally preparing for the next battle in the courtroom in the upcoming days; he would recall Barker to the stand. And this time, he wouldn't just chip at the evidence. He would tear the floor out from under him.

CHAPTER 16 THE GHOST DOMAIN

THE WEEKEND ARRIVED like a truce nobody had formally agreed to.

Friday evening court finished at 4:20 pm — Bluegum unusually prompt, perhaps sensing the jury needed breathing room before the defence dropped its next heavy exhibit on Monday. Avery walked down the Supreme Court steps into late-afternoon heat that still carried the memory of summer.

No reporters rushed him today; the story had moved into a slower, more dangerous phase. People were watching, but they were doing it quietly now.

He drove straight to Rina's place in The Rocks instead of detouring to chambers. When she opened the door Luca was already in pyjamas, damp hair from the bath, clutching a plastic excavator like it was the most important object in the universe.

"Avery!" Luca launched himself forward. Avery caught him under the arms, swung him once in a wide arc that produced the obligatory delighted shriek, then set him down.

"Mate, you're getting heavy. What's your mum feeding you—bricks?"

"Chicken nuggets," Luca announced proudly.

Rina appeared in the hallway, wiping her hands on a tea towel, wearing faded jeans and a soft grey T-shirt that slipped off one shoulder. She didn't say anything at first—just crossed the space between them, rose on her toes, and kissed him properly. Not the quick hello of the past week, but slow and deliberate, the kind of kiss that reminded him the trial hadn't erased everything else.

When she pulled back her eyes searched his face. "You look like you've been carrying bricks too."

"Feels like it." He brushed a thumb along her jaw. "But tomorrow's ours. No court, no files, no Ollie texting me servo stills at 2 am"

She smiled—small, tired, real. "Promise?"

"Cross my heart and hope to die."

Luca tugged at his trouser leg. "We're going to the beach tomorrow?"

"That's the plan, little man."

Rina mouthed thank you over Luca's head.

Saturday morning broke clean and blue. They drove south instead of the usual crowded northern beaches — Cronulla, early enough that the sand was still mostly empty. Luca ran straight for the water with his bucket, shrieking every time a small wave chased his ankles. Rina spread the picnic rug, kicked off her thongs, and sat cross-legged beside Avery while they watched the boy dig an ambitious moat.

For almost forty minutes the world felt ordinary.

Then Avery noticed the man.

Stocky build, navy polo shirt, dark sunglasses, sitting alone two umbrellas down with a newspaper he hadn't turned a page on in ten minutes. Every so often his gaze drifted — casual, practised — toward their rug. When Avery looked directly at him the man lifted the paper again, but not fast enough.

Rina followed Avery's line of sight. Her smile didn't falter but her voice dropped. "Friend of yours?"

"Not exactly."

She reached for the sunscreen bottle, squeezed some into her palm, and rubbed it slowly onto his forearm—mostly an excuse to lean close. "Second one. Over by the kiosk. Grey hoodie, pretending to talk on the phone."

Avery didn't turn. "Same build as the first?"

"Similar. Broad shoulders. Standing like he's waiting for someone who's never going to show."

Luca ran back, sand plastered to wet legs, holding up a perfect spiral shell. "Look! It's a horn shell!"

Rina took it, made the appropriate admiring noises, then glanced at Avery again. The question was in her eyes: how bad is this?

He gave the smallest shake of his head—not here, not in front of the boy.

They ate sandwiches, played an embarrassingly competitive game of beach cricket (Luca won), built a sandcastle that Luca insisted needed a "moat for the sharks". Avery was alert now, but almost paranoid. He was questioning everyday actions with a possible watcher or onlooker: the jogger who looped past three times without breaking stride, the older man in a fishing hat reading the same two pages of a paperback, the woman walking a border collie that never seemed interested in actually walking.

None of them approached. None took photos. They simply existed—this case was starting to pry into his personal life, and he didn't like that.

At 2:30 pm they packed up. Luca fell asleep in the car seat before they reached Botany Road. Rina kept one hand on Avery's thigh the whole drive home, not speaking, just steady pressure.

***

Back at the flat she put Luca down for his nap, then came straight to the living room where Avery stood at the window looking down at the street. A charcoal SUV idled at the kerb opposite, windows tinted, engine running.

Rina stepped behind him, slid her arms around his waist, rested her cheek against his back.

"How long have they been following us?" she asked quietly.

"Since at least Thursday night. Ollie spotted one near the Anchor earlier in the week. Today they stopped pretending to be subtle."

She was silent a moment. "Because of the burners? The map? The signature stuff?"

"And because tomorrow—or Monday rather—I recall Barker and put the enhanced still in front of him. If it's him on that servo footage…" Avery exhaled. "They're not just protecting a project anymore. They're protecting a cop who crossed every line."

Rina turned him gently until they were facing each other.

"You're going to ask the judge for protection?"

"I'm going to ask for Barker to be recalled under subpoena. After that, if the jury sees what I think they'll see, protection orders will come whether I ask or not."

"And us?" She nodded toward the window. "Luca?"

Avery cupped her face. "I've already spoken to Ollie. He's organised a mate—ex-Commonwealth protective service—who's going to sit downstairs tonight and tomorrow night. Plain clothes, no drama. Luca won't even know."

Rina searched his eyes. "And after the trial?"

"After the trial we disappear for a while. Somewhere without mobile coverage. Somewhere nobody can find us unless we want to be found. But moreso, if things go to plan on how I intend, then there'll be no issues anyway. And even then we will still go on a little getaway."

She gave a small, shaky laugh. "You make it sound romantic."

"It will be." He kissed her forehead. "I promise."

***

That night they ordered pizza, put on a Pixar movie Luca had seen six times, and pretended the three of them were just another family on a Saturday evening.

175

Luca fell asleep against Rina's chest halfway through. Avery carried him to bed, then came back to the couch and pulled Rina into his lap.

They didn't speak for a long time—just held each other while the city lights moved across the harbour outside.

But now the world was starting to slow down, Avery's mind started to race faster. He couldn't settle. He stood up and headed toward the dining table, "I need to check something." He told Rina. An eerie feeling was coming together in his mind. The words Barker had said to him, his actions, his behaviour… everything seemed a little off to Avery, and he'd learned to trust his instincts over the years, as they were usually the right call.

Avery sat at the kitchen table, the grainy CCTV stills spread out next to Luca's half-eaten spaghetti. Rina was watching him, her hand resting near the photo of herself and Luca crossing the street.

"You're staring at his legs again," Rina said quietly.

Avery didn't look up. He was holding a magnifying glass over the third burner-phone purchase. "It's the pitch of the body, Rina. Look at the right shoulder. It's hiked higher than the left. He's compensating for a lean."

He grabbed a second photo—a legal tabloid clipping from six months ago showing Detective Jacob Barker walking out of a high-profile sentencing hearing.

"Barker has a lateral meniscus tear from a footy injury in the nineties," Avery muttered, more to himself than her. "I remember him limping during the *R v. Miller* trial. He tries to hide it with a stiff-legged gait, but when he's tired—or in a hurry—the roll comes back."

Avery lined the two photos up. The hooded figure at the convenience store and the Lead Detective in his Sunday best.

"The height marker in the shop says 183 centimetres. Barker is six-foot-one on his service file. The shoulder roll is identical. I've seen it up close in court. The way he tucks his chin into his collar to hide his jawline..."

Avery's blood ran cold. "It's not just a coincidence. The man who 'failed' to find the burner-phone buyer is the man who bought them."

Rina leaned in, her voice trembling. "Avery, if Barker is the one in the hoodie, then he didn't just 'miss' the evidence. He's been standing in the courtroom every day watching you try to find *him*."

The realisation hit him like a physical blow.

"He's not just the lead investigator," Avery whispered. "He's involved."

They sat in silence. Rina knew the best way to steal his attention back was with patience. Avery finally returned to earth when Rina broke the silence.

Eventually she whispered against his neck, "I'm not scared of them watching us."

"No?"

"I'm scared of what happens if you win—and they decide the only way to stop the story is to stop you."

Avery tightened his arms. "They won't get the chance."

She lifted her head, eyes fierce in the dim light. "You don't get to be the only one making promises tonight. If anything happens to you, I will burn this city down looking for who did it. Understand?"

He smiled—small, fierce, matching hers. "Understood."

They stayed like that until the movie credits rolled and the room was quiet except for the low hum of the fridge and the distant wash of traffic.

Outside, the charcoal SUV was still parked across the street.

Inside, for a few more hours, they were safe.

But the weekend was ending.

Monday morning the courtroom would open again.

And when it did, Avery would stop chipping at the edges.

He would swing.

THE COURTROOM FELT quieter than it had in days. The public gallery was still packed, but the energy had shifted from electric anticipation to something more watchful—reporters sat with notebooks instead of frantic typing, legal observers lingered in the back rows, and the jury filed in looking thoughtful, some already flipping back to the burner map and domain slides from earlier in the week. They were no longer just absorbing; they were waiting, piecing things together. There was also an eerie presence of watchful onlookers that Avery hadn't noticed before. He had usually been familiar with the faces of the reporters, but these people weren't reporters. Some of these were well-built, some of these were old and attentive, all men in suits.

Avery rose. "Your Honour, the defence calls has witnesses to recall, but first, we seek leave to tender additional documentary evidence arising from ongoing investigation—specifically, supplementary CCTV stills and clerk statements related to the burner phone purchases already admitted. These materials are authenticated and go to the alternative motive already before the jury."

Turner rose. "Objection—late tender. The Crown has closed its case. This is new evidence without proper foundation."

"Your Honour, the materials are from the same service station and stores referenced in Mr Patel's recall testimony. They are authenticated by the clerks and CCTV providers. They are limited to visual identification of the purchaser and timing, and are highly probative of reasonable doubt. The defence has been diligent; the images were enhanced and statements obtained only yesterday."

Bluegum considered. "The evidence relates to material already admitted. Leave is granted for tender, limited to identification and timing. The jury will be directed."

Avery tendered the bundle: three grainy CCTV stills and matching clerk statements. The projector lit up.

Avery was allowed to recall Mr Patel to the stand.

Thankfully, Mr Patel was only working in the same vicinity, so logistically he was able to attend on such short notice. This was so he could once again confirm the burner phone locations geographically, but link it back to the case at hand and introduce it to the jury. Carefully, but succinctly, Avery also drew the attention of the jury back to the mysterious messages that Elle received, both confirmed by Sophie and Mr Patel.

"These are the purchase moments for the three burners," Avery said, voice calm. "The first two—'*Call me*' six weeks prior and '*Elle, this is serious…*' two weeks prior—show a man in a dark hoodie, face obscured, paying cash. The third—'*we need to talk*' on the night of the murder—shows the same man, same build, same hoodie, same posture. The clerks confirm exact change, no chit-chat, male, mid-forties, dark hair."

The jury leaned forward. The older man in the back row adjusted his glasses. The front-row woman made a note, her pen moving slowly.

Avery advanced to a side-by-side comparison. "Note the height marker on the servo door: approximately 183 cm. The man's gait—slight favouring of the left leg. The way he tucks his chin when paying. These are consistent across all three purchases…"

Turner rose for cross on the tender. "Objection! Relevance again, Your Honour? Mr Patel is here as an expert witness on phone analysis, not CCTV examination."

"You're absolutely correct, my apologies Your Honour, I was just about to ask Mr Patel to confirm that this close-up of the still is in fact the same still from the CCTV footage just to show the jury that this footage hasn't been tampered with, and simply ask Mr Patel to corroborate the timestamps of the purchase."

"That's enough Mr Santos. The jury will ignore the last remarks made by counsel. Mr Santos, I am giving you one last warning, or this witness will be excused."

Turner sat. No further damage.

"Mr Patel, can you once again confirm from what you previously found, that these messages came from these very burner phones purchased right here on this CCTV footage?"

"Yes, assuming what you're showing me hasn't been tampered with, and the serials match with what the clerks told you, then yes that would be the buyer of the burner phones."

"Thank you." Avery returned to his seat.

"Redirect, Your Honour." Turner stood firmly. "Mr Patel. Even if, and that's a huge *if* the buyer of these burner phones is the same buyer, do you have any proof that this was the same person who sent the text messages to the victim?"

"No, there is no evidence showing that."

"And beyond all of that, even *if* this buyer did text the victim, were any of these burner phones located on or around the scene of the crime on the night of the murder of Elle Stanis?"

"No, again there's no evidence supporting that."

"So, Mr Patel, is there even any evidence linking this burner to the actual crime we are trying here?"

"Objection!"

"No further questions, Your Honour."

Bluegum directed the jury: "This evidence is admitted solely to assist you in assessing whether there is a reasonable possibility of another motive or explanation. It is not evidence that any particular person purchased these phones or committed the offence."

The jury absorbed it in silence. A few exchanged glances; the woman in the front row looked at the stills, then at Avery, her expression shifting from curiosity to something closer to unease.

***

Bluegum adjourned after the long Court day, a jury member had not returned after lunch due to some form of nausea and diarrhoea – a lunch break that stole the afternoon from the lawyers, and from Kristof. Avery thought about this, but also thought that this little blessing would give him more time for his case, and he would take any extra second he could get.

In the corridor Ollie was waiting—unusually still, arms folded, eyes sharp.

Avery stepped out. "The stills landed. Jury's looking at the gait."

Ollie didn't smile. He handed Avery a slim envelope. "Tech just finished the enhancement run on the third purchase—the *'we need to talk'* burner. They pulled a partial side-profile frame from the second camera angle. Not enough for facial recognition, but enough for body comparison."

Avery opened the envelope. Inside was a single enhanced still: the man in the hoodie, head turned slightly toward the door as he left the service station. The jawline, the set of the shoulders, the way the left hand tucked into the pocket—familiar.

Ollie's voice was low. "It's Barker."

Avery stared at the image. The grey at the temples was hidden under the hood, but the posture, the slight limp on the left, the way he carried himself—twenty years on the job left marks that enhancement couldn't erase. Avery's theory was confirmed, but his own conclusive jump would not be enough in the courtroom, he needed more and was hoping Ollie could provide.

"You're sure?"

"Cross-checked with his service photos and CCTV from the court precinct last week. Same gait, same shoulder roll. Same height. It's him."

Avery exhaled slowly. "He bought the burners. He sent the messages. He pressured her."

Ollie nodded. "And he's the lead detective. If he's tied to Greyrock—or someone inside it—he had motive to steer the investigation. Frame Kristof, close the file, keep Elle quiet forever."

Avery folded the envelope and slipped it into his briefcase. "We don't accuse yet. We recall him tomorrow with this. Let the jury see him dodge again. Let them connect it themselves."

Ollie's eyes were hard. "Watch your back, mate. Barker knows we're close. He was parked near Rina's flat again last night. Not subtle."

Avery's jaw tightened. "He's scared. Good. Means we're right. Is your friend still on watch?"

"Yes, all secure. Just keeping you in the loop."

He stepped outside into the midday sun on Phillip Street. The harbour glittered, sharp and indifferent. Avery felt the case tilting—not just toward doubt, but toward exposure. Barker wasn't just a hostile witness anymore. He was a suspect.

He pulled out his phone and texted Rina: Got a breakthrough. Jury's noticing the gaps. Coming home for lunch. Stay inside until I get there.

Her reply came fast: *Waiting for you my love. Be careful xx*

He pocketed the phone and started walking, the envelope in his briefcase feeling heavier than any exhibit so far. Tomorrow, he would recall Barker. And this time, the questions wouldn't be gentle.

THE FOLLOWING DAY in the courtroom, Avery recognised the same eerie men he noticed previously. He looked directly at each and every one of them this time. They sat too still, shoulders squared like men used to standing at attention. Greyrock security? Private investigators? Or just muscle sent to remind everyone that some lines weren't meant to be crossed?

The jury filed in looking heavier than previously—notebooks already open to the burner map, the gait comparison stills, the red circle that had refused to fade from their minds over the weekend.

"All rise."

Justice Bluegum settled onto the bench with the same measured calm he'd shown for three weeks. If he sensed the atmosphere had turned electric, he gave no sign.

"Mr Santos," he said, "the defence may proceed."

Avery rose. He buttoned his jacket once—slow, deliberate—then walked to the centre of the bar table.

No notes. No lectern. Just him and the envelope Ollie had slipped him that morning.

"Your Honour, the defence recalls Detective Jacob Barker for further cross-examination."

A ripple moved through the gallery—soft, but unmistakable. Turner was on his feet before the words finished landing.

"Objection. The Crown closed its case. Detective Barker has already been extensively cross-examined. This is an attempt to re-open the Prosecution's evidence under the guise of rebuttal."

Bluegum looked at Avery. "Mr Santos?"

"Your Honour, new material has come to light since Detective Barker's original testimony—material directly relevant to the alternative motive theory already before the jury. The defence seeks leave to recall him for limited questions on that material only. The probative value outweighs any prejudice, and the interests of justice require it."

Turner's voice sharpened. "What 'new material'? The defence has been drip-feeding speculation for days—Greyrock, burners, forged signatures. This is ambush."

Bluegum considered for a long moment. His eyes flicked to the back of the gallery, to Avery, to Turner, then back to Avery.

"Leave is granted," he said finally. "Limited to the new material foreshadowed in the defence opening and developed through prior witnesses. The jury will be reminded of the limited purpose. Detective Barker may be recalled."

Turner sat slowly, jaw tight. The associate called for Barker.

The side door opened. Barker entered—dark jacket, tie knotted like a noose, face carved from stone. He took the oath without looking at Avery, eyes fixed on the witness box rail as if it were the only thing keeping him upright.

Avery approached the lectern. He placed the envelope on it—unopened for now—and let the silence stretch.

"Detective Barker," he began, voice level, "you were the lead investigator on the death of Elle Stanis. You attended the scene at 4:15 am on 13 March last year. You arrested Mr Stanis that afternoon. You conducted the formal interview. Correct?"

"Yes."

"You described this as a classic domestic homicide—rage, jealousy, a husband who couldn't let go of his wife's affair."

Barker's jaw flexed. "That's what the evidence showed."

Avery nodded once. "And part of that evidence was three messages received by Elle Stanis in the weeks before her death. *'Call me.' 'Elle, this is serious, I am sorry but let me explain.'* And on the night she died—*'we need to talk.'* You were aware of those messages during your investigation?"

"Yes."

"You obtained the phone records. You knew they came from three different prepaid numbers, purchased with cash, no subscriber details."

"Yes."

"Were you able to identify who purchased these burner phones?"

"No."

"Your Honour, the defence would like to exhibit these as impeachment evidence." Avery opened the envelope. He removed the three CCTV stills—the originals from Friday, plus the enhanced side-profile from the third purchase—and tendered them as exhibits.

"These are stills from the purchase locations of those three burners. The clerks have confirmed the buyer: male, mid-forties, dark hair, paying exact change. The height marker puts him at approximately 183 centimetres. Note the slight favouring of the left leg when he walks. The way he tucks his chin when he pays.

The posture—shoulders rolled forward, left hand in pocket."

He advanced the slides. Side-by-side comparison. Then the enhanced frame: partial profile, jawline clear under the hood.

Barker's eyes flicked to the screen. His hands, resting on the rail, tightened until the knuckles blanched white.

Avery let the image sit.

"Detective, do you have any reason to lie about purchasing these burner phones?"

Turner shot up. "Objection! For a number of reasons, Your Honour! Counsel is badgering the witness. No foundation. This is not identification evidence—it's an invitation to the jury to play detective. The man in these photographs may not even be Detective Barker, and he is ambushing the jury! Counsel is attempting to get a mistrial!"

The courtroom erupted.

The judge ordered silence, and ordered the jury out of the room whilst the judge spoke to both lawyers in chambers.

***

"Mr Santos! What on earth is this? I have given you plenty of rope to make your defence, and I am inclined to say that you are looking like you are hanging yourself with it–"

"Your Honour, I –"

"I am not finished. This is not an expedition, we are trying the case against your client who has been charged with murdering his wife, and I will not sit by whilst you attempt to make a mockery of this Court and the system."

Avery waited until there was complete silence.

"Your Honour, if I may," Avery paused to ensure the judge was finished before explaining, "thank you, Your Honour. However, I am not making a mockery of this Court. I said from the start that I would show everyone that my client is innocent of these charges and we will

195

bring the guilty ones out of the shadows and into the light. Now, my own investigator and I were able to dig some very conflicting evidence that not only presents that the real killer could be someone else, but it also shows that the detectives were derelict in their duty to investigate the case. On top of that, Your Honour, if the lead investigator of the case, happens to be the one obstructing justice and potentially framing my client, then he we have an even bigger problem here."

Turner tried to interject, but the judge held a hand up to him whilst he pondered a response.

"This may be the case, if there was any hard evidence pointing to what you're alluding to Mr Santos." Bluegum said bluntly, "but from where I am sitting, it does only look like a tactic made to distract."

"These photographs, Your Honour." Avery firmly slapped them on the desk of Justice Bluegum. "This is not a distraction. This is Detective Jacob Barker, and we have him right there on the stand right now… Your

Honour, you've let me recall him to the stand for this purpose."

Before the judge he let the lawyers go, he called in Detective Barker into chambers.

***

When the judge and both lawyers returned to the courtroom, the silence felt heavier, as though the air itself had thickened with the weight of what had just been argued behind closed doors.

Justice Bluegum took his seat without flourish. He adjusted his robes, glanced briefly at the jury—who had been brought back in and now sat unnaturally still— then fixed his gaze on the witness box.

"Members of the jury," he began, voice deliberate and carrying the quiet authority that had kept this trial on track for weeks, "during your absence the Court heard submissions from counsel regarding objections to certain questions and the tender of photographs. I have ruled as follows."

He paused, letting the jury absorb that they had missed nothing trivial.

"The photographs—exhibits D-45 to D-47—are admitted into evidence. They are admitted solely for the limited purpose of assisting you in determining whether there is a reasonable possibility of an alternative motive or explanation for the death of Elle Stanis, as that possibility has already been raised in the defence case. You must not treat these images as positive identification of any particular person, including Detective Barker. They are grainy, partial, and lack facial features. Any resemblance to any individual is a matter for you to assess carefully, but only as part of the overall circumstantial picture already before you. You must not speculate or draw any adverse inference against Detective Barker personally unless the evidence properly and fairly supports it."

He turned his head slightly toward Barker, who remained rigid in the witness box.

"Detective Barker has claimed the privilege against self-incrimination in respect of certain questions that might tend to expose him to criminal liability in other proceedings. Where I have been satisfied that the claim is properly made, I have issued a certificate under section 128 of the Evidence Act. That means any answer given under such a certificate—and any evidence obtained as a direct consequence of that answer—cannot be used against Detective Barker in any future criminal Prosecution. You must not draw any adverse inference from the fact that the privilege was claimed or that a certificate was issued. It is a protection provided by law and says nothing about guilt or innocence in this trial."

Bluegum let that settle. Several jurors exchanged quick glances; one woman in the front row pressed her lips together tightly.

"Mr Santos," the judge said, "you may continue your cross-examination. Confine yourself strictly to the photographs and their relevance to the alternative-motive case. No further questions that directly invite the witness to incriminate himself without foundation."

Avery rose again. He kept his tone even, almost conversational, as though the chambers drama had never happened.

"Detective Barker," he said, "looking at exhibit D-47—the enhanced still from the third burner purchase on the night of 12 March—do you see any similarity between the build, posture, and gait of the man shown and your own physical characteristics?"

Barker's eyes flicked to the screen. He took a slow breath.

"I see a man in a hoodie," he said flatly. "The image is low resolution. I cannot say there is any meaningful similarity."

Avery nodded once, as though the answer was expected.

"And the height marker visible in the doorway—approximately 183 centimetres—does that accord with your recorded height on your NSW Police service file?"

Turner rose halfway. "Objection—calls for confirmation of personnel records not in evidence."

"Objection allowed," Bluegum said. "Move on, Mr Santos."

Avery shifted ground smoothly.

"Detective, during your investigation, did you make any inquiries into whether the purchaser of these three burners might have had a connection to the Marrickville development project or to Greyrock Developments?"

Barker's jaw tightened fractionally.

"We investigated all lines of inquiry that appeared relevant. No credible connection to any third party emerged."

"That's not quite what I asked," Avery said quietly. "Did you personally make, or direct anyone to make, any inquiries into a possible link between the burner purchaser and Greyrock?"

A long pause.

"No specific inquiries were directed to that entity."

Avery let the answer sit.

"No further questions at this time, Your Honour."

He returned to his seat.

Kristof leaned in, voice barely audible. "Did he just admit he didn't look?"

Avery gave the smallest nod. "He didn't deny it either."

Turner rose for re-examination. He kept it short, surgical. "Detective Barker, did you at any time purchase any of the prepaid phones referred to in these photographs?"

"No."

"Did you send any messages to Elle Stanis from any phone?"

"No."

"Did you have any involvement in her death or in what defence are claiming as *framing* Kristof Stanis?"

"No."

"Do you think Mr Stanis was framed?"

"No."

"What do you think then, Detective?"

"Mr Stanis killed his wife." Barker answered swiftly, and firmly, with a commanding presence that weighed on the jury.

Turner sat. The questions were blunt, the answers immediate. But the jury had already heard the silences that came before them.

Bluegum glanced at the clock.

"We will adjourn until 2:15 pm Members of the jury, the usual reminders apply. Do not discuss the case, do not make any independent inquiries, and do not form any conclusions until all the evidence is in and I have directed you on the law."

"All rise."

As the jury filed out, several looked back—not at Kristof, not at Avery, but at the witness box where Barker still stood, unmoving. The older man in the back row shook his head once, slowly. The woman in the front row kept her eyes on the now-dark screen a moment longer than necessary.

Ollie and Avery met for lunch to debrief. "He didn't crack," Ollie said quietly. "But he didn't have to. The jury heard what they needed to hear. The silences spoke louder than the denials."

Avery exhaled slowly. "Turner's re-examination was smart—short, clean. But we've got the certificate on record now. If Barker ever faces his own charges, those answers are locked away. And the jury knows he needed protection to give them."

Kristof was escorted past in the distance. He caught Avery's eye through the glass and gave a single, firm nod—gratitude, hope, something close to belief.

Avery returned it.

"We close tomorrow," he said to Ollie. "Did you secure the gait expert? We have him first thing…"

"Yes, he's here."

"Good, we lead with him, then summation. I need more though. I still feel like there's a missing connection. No more fireworks—just the facts they can't unsee."

Ollie glanced toward the stairwell where Barker had already disappeared, flanked by two uniforms who hadn't been there earlier.

"He's not going anywhere quiet," Ollie murmured.

"Professional Standards will have him by close of play today. LECC too, probably."

Avery's phone buzzed. Rina: *Court feed is going wild. You okay? Luca wants to know if the "bad dragon" is in jail yet.*

He smiled—small, tired, real—and typed back: *Dragon's cornered. Tell Luca we're winning. Home tonight. Love you both.*

Her reply came instantly: *We love you more. Door's open. Come straight here—no detours.*

He pocketed the phone and looked down the long marble corridor. The suits from the gallery were gone, but the echo of their presence lingered.

Tomorrow the defence would close. Tomorrow the jury would begin to deliberate. The game clock is ticking for Avery, but he knew he had won one of the most important battles.

And somewhere in the city, a lead detective who had once walked into every room like he owned it would be wondering how much longer he could keep walking free.

CHAPTER 19 THE BEAR

THE ADJOURNMENT HIT like a gavel strike, the courtroom emptying in a controlled rush that left Avery standing at the bar table, heart pounding not from the drama but from the quiet certainty that the pieces were finally aligning. Barker had been excused, his denials hanging in the air like smoke, but the jury's glances—those told the real story. They weren't just doubting the Crown anymore; they were questioning everything.

Ollie was waiting outside as usual, but holding a tense stillness. He handed Avery a flat white without the customary banter, his eyes scanning the milling crowd—reporters, clerks, the eerie suits slipping away like shadows.

"That certificate's going to haunt him," Ollie said low. "Professional Standards is already sniffing around. I heard whispers from a mate in the internal affairs PSC—Barker's phone logs are under subpoena as we speak."

Avery took a sip, the bitterness grounding him. "He didn't crack on the stand, but he knows we're close. The limp, the height—it's too much coincidence. And if he bought those burners…"

Ollie glanced around once more, then pulled a slim folder from his jacket. "It's more than the burners now. I dug deeper last night, cross-referenced Elle's council access logs with Barker's duty roster. Remember the affair the Crown keeps hammering? The 'jealous husband' motive?"

Avery's pulse quickened. "What about it?"

Ollie opened the folder, revealing printouts: timestamped emails, blurred security footage from a Marrickville council building, and a redacted report from a discreet PI Avery had Ollie hire weeks ago. "Elle's lover wasn't some random colleague or old flame. It was Barker."

The words landed like a punch. Avery stared at the top page—a photo of Barker and Elle in a parked car near the council offices, timestamped two months before the murder. Close, intimate, her hand on his arm, his face turned toward hers in a way that spoke volumes.

The photo was actually found by pure luck. Sometimes the universe will lend its helping hand. Turns out that PI had tracked previous locations of Elle, and mostly were following her routine through work and home, and the occasional café or shopping centre visit. However, there she frequented over a time, which at first was overlooked. This was because the hotel in the city would share a carpark with the council offices, so Elle parking in there seemed nothing out of the ordinary.

The PI happened to have a cousin who was front desk manager of that same who could help pull up camera recordings and video footage dating months back. Out of sheer luck, they were able to just find one photo of them in the car with the camera overlooking. Given, that it was just the one photo, it would seem that Detective Barker knew how to hide himself. But everyone makes mistakes and slip ups. This time, this helped Avery and his client.

"You're sure?" Avery asked, though he already knew the answer. Ollie didn't bring half-baked intel.

"Positive. The PI looked into all the movements of Elle leading up to her death, which got him on a what he thought would be a goose chase on Barker…"

"How'd he get from Elle to Barker?"

"Well, he's an ex-cop from QLD who's been quietly following the case too – he said something about Barker's reactions and over-investment in the case from day one. Apparently, Barker went to the hotel Elle used to park in. Being city parking, he thought nothing of it initially, but upon further investigating he was able to find that photo. But it gets worse. Or better, depending on how you look at it." Ollie flipped to the next page: a chain of emails from a Greyrock Developments executive to an anonymous account traced back to Barker's personal IP. "Greyrock planted him. Hired him off-books six months before the affair started. The job?

Get close to Elle, use her position on the development approvals committee to flip the denial on their Marrickville project. Seduce her if necessary—whatever it took to get inside info and leverage."

"You got all this from the tech guy?"

"Yeah, that reminds me – he wants double fee this time."

"What, why? Actually, whatever. Pay him" Avery would normally question these sudden raise in prices, but in this moment his attention was too focused on the Barker details.

Avery exhaled slowly, piecing it together. "So, it wasn't love at first sight. It was a setup. Barker worms his way in, starts the affair to gain her trust, pressures her to overturn the denial. But something went wrong— maybe she refused, or threatened to expose him. And Greyrock… they didn't want loose ends."

Ollie nodded grimly. "Explains the burners too. He wasn't just texting as a lover; he was escalating the pressure. *'Call me.' 'This is serious.' 'We need to talk.'* All while steering the investigation away from Greyrock after she turned up dead."

The noise faded around them as they continued their pace away from the Courtroom and into the nearby park bench. Avery felt the case reshape in his mind: not a domestic rage killing, but a corporate hit dressed up as one, with a corrupt cop at the centre pulling strings to frame Kristof.

Avery murmured. "That explains why he was lead detective. He probably pushed his way onto the case."

"Arrogance," Ollie said. "Or desperation. Greyrock's project was worth billions—council denial could've sunk it. We couldn't find anything on Barker – no pay offs nothing – but Greyrock probably dangled a payoff he couldn't refuse or they have something on him. Man was decorated in the force for years."

Avery closed the folder, mind racing. This was the twist—the crack that could shatter the entire Prosecution. But using it meant exposing Barker fully, and Greyrock wouldn't let that slide quietly.

His phone buzzed. Unknown number.

You've poked the bear. Pull back now, or the ones you love pay first.

Avery showed Ollie, who swore under his breath. "They know we're onto this. Rina and Luca—move them tonight. Hospice for her mum, like we discussed. And those bikie favours? Call them in now."

This was probably one of the times that Avery appreciated his years of defence work – he'd successfully built up a network of "friends" who he could turn to in emergent situations like this.

Avery nodded, deleting the message. "We don't stop. But we get careful. Tomorrow, the gait expert plants the final seeds. Then summation. If Barker's the affair partner, the jury will connect the dots themselves."

Kristof was led past in cuffs, catching Avery's eye. For the first time, there was real hope in his gaze—not fragile, but steel-edged. It was all starting to make sense… in a way. Someone else was to blame for his wife's death. He didn't know the exact reasons but now that there's someone else who's been hiding in the shadows and dragged into the spotlight, for the world to see, Kristof is also finally starting to see the world again.

***

Avery returned to the courtroom for the afternoon session, the folder tucked away like dynamite. The contest wasn't just about acquittal anymore. It was about dragging the truth into the light, no matter who got burned.

Outside, the harbour wind picked up, carrying the faint tang of rain. Shadows lengthened on Phillip Street.

And somewhere in the city, a detective who had crossed every line was starting to feel the walls close in.

CHAPTER 20 THE PHOTO

THE AFTERNOON SESSION ended almost before it began. Justice Bluegum glanced at the clock, noted the defence's final witness—the gait analyst—was not yet available due to a delayed flight from Melbourne, and asked the parties if they consented to an early adjournment. Turner had no objection; Avery certainly didn't. The jury was released with the usual reminders, looking a little relieved to escape the heavy atmosphere that had settled over Courtroom 11 since Barker's recall.

"All rise."

The courtroom emptied in its familiar rhythm. Avery packed his notes slowly, letting the others file out first. Kristof caught his eye from the dock as the guards led him away—quiet, steady gratitude in the nod he gave. Avery returned it, but his mind was already outside these walls.

In the corridor, Ollie fell into step beside him. No flat white this time; the ritual felt too ordinary for the weight pressing down.

"Gait expert's confirmed for 10 am tomorrow," Ollie said. "Flight lands at 8:30. He'll go straight to chambers to prep. I've got the final report printed and ready to tender."

Avery nodded absently. "Good. But we're not waiting until morning for everything else."

Ollie read his tone. "The photo from earlier?"

"Among other things." Avery pulled out his phone, opened the deleted-message folder where he'd archived the image of Rina and Luca crossing the street. He stared at it again—the backpack label, Luca's small hand swallowed in Rina's, the telephoto compression that made the shot feel invasive, predatory. "They're not just watching. They're showing me they can reach them anytime."

Ollie's voice dropped. "Bikies are in position. Two arrived an hour ago—big lads, quiet. One's parked two streets over in an unmarked Commodore. The other's on foot near the corner shop. Third one's due in twenty. Are you sure you don't want me to call your brother?"

Ollie knew better than to bring this up. Avery's brother was typically a topic that is off limits, but in this scenario Ollie thought he might see reason.

"No. Stick with the guys we have."

"Okay, well they'll rotate through the night. No one gets close without us knowing."

Avery exhaled. "And the hospice?"

"Paperwork's signed. Ambulance transfer at 7 am tomorrow—discreet, no sirens. Rina's mum will be in a private room by breakfast. Rina and Luca can follow in your car if you want, or I'll drive them. Your call."

"I'll drive them," Avery said without hesitation. "I want to see them settled."

They stepped out into Phillip Street. The rain that had threatened earlier was falling steadily now—cold, persistent, turning the footpaths slick and reflective. Avery pulled up his collar, scanned the street out of habit. No charcoal SUV, no obvious tails. But the absence felt deliberate, like a predator going quiet before the strike.

His phone buzzed again. Unknown number.

This time, no photo. Just text.

Meet me. Alone. Pier 26, Rozelle Bay. 9 pm tonight. Come without your shadow. That includes the bikies.

Avery showed the screen to Ollie.

Ollie's eyes narrowed. "Rozelle Bay. My boat's moored two berths down from there. Coincidence?"

"Or bait," Avery said. "It's Barker. Has to be. He's cornered, knows LECC is circling, knows we've got the affair photo and the Greyrock link. He wants to talk—maybe confess, maybe threaten, maybe something in between."

"You're not going alone."

"I have to." Avery met Ollie's gaze. "If he's willing to meet, he's close to breaking. One push, and he might give us what we need: on-record confirmation that… anything, whatever showing that Kristof didn't do this. That's reasonable doubt on steroids. But if I show up with muscle—or you—he'll bolt."

Ollie didn't like it. "At least let me shadow from the boat. Binoculars, no contact. If it goes south—"

"If it goes south, you'll hear about it." Avery pocketed the phone. "But this is my play. Get Rina and Luca ready. I'll be home in an hour to help pack. Then I'll head to the pier after they're safe."

Ollie studied him for a long beat. "You sure about this?"

"No," Avery admitted. "But I'm sure we can't keep waiting for them to make the next move."

They parted at the steps—Ollie heading toward the carpark to coordinate, Avery hailing a taxi. The ride to the flat was quiet, rain drumming on the roof like impatient fingers.

Rina opened the door, Luca already in pyjamas, eating an early dinner at the kitchen table. She took one look at Avery's face and knew.

"What happened?"

"Got another one."

"Another message?" she asked softly.

He nodded, stepped inside, closed the door. Luca waved a forkful of spaghetti. "Hey, Avery! Want some? It's got extra cheese!"

Avery managed a smile. "In a minute, my man." He turned to Rina, voice low. "I have to go out tonight. Late. Ollie's people are here—three of them, good ones. They'll stay close until morning. You and Luca pack what you need. We leave at six for the hospice. I'll drive."

Her eyes searched his. "Where are you going?"

"Meeting someone who might end this. Alone."

"Barker?"

He didn't deny it. "If he's ready to talk, it could change everything tomorrow."

"And if he's not?" Her voice stayed level, but the fear was there, quiet and sharp.

"Then I walk away. But I need you safe first." He reached for her hand. "I'm coming back."

She wanted to protest, but knew it would not change the events. Avery would only go if he knew he needed to. And she knew this, so she submitted. She squeezed once, hard. "Be safe please."

Luca finished his dinner, oblivious, chattering about the Lego castle he wanted to finish before bed. Avery sat with him, helped add a final tower, listened to the boy explain how the dragon would never get past the moat. Normal sounds in an abnormal night.

***

After Luca brushed his teeth and climbed into bed with a story, Avery and Rina stood in the hallway.

"Promise me," she said. "No heroics. If it feels wrong, you leave."

"I promise." He kissed her—slow, deliberate, tasting of rain and worry and everything they hadn't said yet. "I love you both. Lock the door behind me. Ollie's guys are outside. Text me if anything feels off."

She nodded, eyes fierce. "We'll be ready at six. Come home."

He stepped out into the rain, pulled up his collar, and walked toward the waiting Commodore where one of the bikies—plain clothes, no nonsense—gave him a small nod from the driver's seat.

The night was long, the city wet and watchful.

At 9 pm, Pier 26 waited in the dark.

THE RAIN HAD eased to a fine mist by the time Avery reached Pier 26. Rozelle Bay was quiet at this hour—moored yachts rocking gently, the water black and glassy under sodium lights. The pier itself was a long concrete finger jutting into the bay, lined with bollards and coiled ropes, empty except for the occasional security lamp throwing weak yellow pools.

Avery walked slowly, hands loose at his sides, collar turned up against the damp. No phone in hand; he'd left it in the car two blocks away, screen dark. Ollie had argued against that too, but Avery needed Barker to believe he'd come alone. Trust, or at least the illusion of it, was the only leverage he had left.

Halfway down the pier, a figure detached from the shadow of a steel piling. Tall, broad-shouldered, the familiar limp more pronounced now that he wasn't performing for a courtroom. Barker stepped into the light—dark jacket zipped to the chin, hood up, hands in pockets. One hand stayed low, the outline of something solid pressing against the fabric.

Avery stopped ten metres away. Close enough to talk. Far enough to react if it came to that.

"You came," Barker said. Voice rough, like he hadn't used it in hours. "Thought you might bring your pet investigator. Or those bikie mates you've got circling the flat."

Avery kept his tone even. "I'm alone. Like you asked."

Barker gave a short, humourless laugh. "Smart. Or stupid. Hard to tell anymore."

They stood in silence for a beat, only the lap of water and the distant hum of city traffic. Barker's right hand eased out of the pocket—slowly, deliberately—revealing the matte black grip of a Glock. Not raised, not yet. Just held low, barrel down, like a man deciding whether the conversation was worth the bullet.

"You should have left it alone, Santos, I told you not to poke the bear. I warned you about them." Barker said quietly. "Come here."

Barker held up the gun, and forced Avery to walk closer. He proceeded to pat him down to ensure he wasn't armed and wasn't being recorded. He took Avery's phone and switched it off.

"I came here to kill you, you know."

"For what? Discovering the truth?"

"You think you have, but you haven't even scratched the surface."

"I have an idea. And it all leads back to Greyrock."

"Greyrock… they're not like the usual scumbags you defend. They don't threaten. They act. Quietly. Cleanly. No loose ends. You keep digging, and the next photo won't be your girlfriend crossing the street. It'll be her funeral. Or the kid's."

Avery felt the words land like stones in his gut, but he didn't flinch. "You sent the photo."

"Wasn't me." Barker's jaw tightened. "That was their way of saying hello. I'm just the messenger who's out of moves… That's why I changed my mind actually." Barker held up his phone, showing the same photo of Rina and Luca. "I didn't take the photo. But I was sent it. And that means they've told me to deal with this problem. And if I don't they'll send the next guy in…"

"Then why meet me? To warn me?" Avery asked. "If you're still their dog, why risk this?"

Barker looked out over the water, the gun still loose in his hand. "Because I'm tired. Because every night I see her face—Elle's. And those kids… when I saw the photo of Rina and Luca, it reminded me of this." Barker pulled up a picture from his phone. In a very similar sight, Elle was crossing the street with her two kids. "I received this photo from them the day she before she was killed. I didn't do anything to stop it back then, but maybe I could do the right thing now."

Barker continued soberly, "the way she looked at me when she realised what I'd done. Started as a job. Get close, get the intel, flip the vote. Greyrock paid well. I had debts… bad ones. Thought I could keep it clean. Then I fell for her. Real. Stupid. Real."

He turned back to Avery, eyes hollow under the hood.

"She found out. Found out I had forged her signature and approved the tender. Confronted me the weeks before she died. Eventually said she was going to the police, to the council integrity unit. I begged her not to. Told her they'd ruin us both. She wouldn't listen. Said she couldn't live with it."

Avery took one careful step forward. "So, you killed her."

Barker's grip tightened on the gun. For a second, Avery thought that was it—the barrel coming up, the flash, the end. But Barker instead didn't fire his gun, he hit him right on the head. Avery stumbled from the heavy blow, blood starting leak from a small gash on the top right of his forehead.

"I would never hurt her."

The words hung there, raw.

"I loved her," Barker said. "More than the job, more than the money, more than staying out of prison. When she turned up dead… I knew it who it was. Greyrock doesn't leave witnesses. They sent someone. Professional. No trace. Then they leaned on me to steer the investigation. Frame the husband. Close the file. Make it look domestic. And I did because I was scared. Because if I didn't, they'd come for me next. And because part of me thought… maybe Kristof deserved it for cheating on her first."

Avery let the silence stretch. "You framed an innocent man."

Barker's laugh was bitter. "Innocent? He was screwing around behind her back. He may not have killed her, but he is the reason she is dead… Too late. Why do you think it was easier for me to get close to her in the first place. He had already hurt her, and was continuing to hurt her."

The gun dipped lower, almost to his side.

"Why tell me this?" Avery asked.

"Because you're going to win tomorrow anyway,"

Barker said. "The trial, the stills, the jury's already smelling blood. LECC is closing in. My career's over. Might as well burn it all down on my terms."

He looked at Avery, eyes steady for the first time. "I'll come to court tomorrow. I'll take the stand again—if the judge allows it. I'll say what I just said. No certificate this time. Full exposure. But you have to promise me one thing."

"What?"

"Protect my Elle's family. I don't have any kids and even though she ended things with me – I know for a fact that she loved those kids more than anything."

"And what about Greyrock – they'll kill you for all this."

"You're right, they probably will. These people aren't the ones you mess around with."

"If you get on the stand tomorrow, I will do everything in my power to protect you."

Barker laughed at the thought. "Ha! You mean your little bikie boys and that pesky investigator? Mate, you don't even know the level you're dealing with."

Avery studied him. The man in front of him wasn't the stone-faced detective anymore. Just a broken cop who'd crossed every line and found nothing on the other side.

Barker stated, "Elle's kids, they'll go back to their dad. But for the rest of their lives you need to stay watching. No one else can find out about Greyrock. Anyone you tell, you risk putting in danger. So, you keep everything to yourself."

"I'll make sure Ollie's people watch them too," Avery said. "But if you're lying—if this is a setup—"

"It's not." Barker holstered the gun slowly, deliberately, sliding it back into his waistband. "I'm done lying."

He turned to walk away, then paused. "One more thing. Elle… she never stopped loving Kristof. Even after everything. She left me. That bastard did not deserve her."

Barker disappeared into the mist, limp fading into the dark.

Avery stood there a long time, rain dripping from his hair, the weight of the confession settling like lead.

He walked back to the car, started the engine, and drove toward the flat.

CHAPTER 22 INNOCENT

Avery stood motionless on the pier long after Barker's silhouette had dissolved into the mist. The rain had picked up again, steady now, drumming on the concrete and running in thin rivers toward the black water. His head throbbed where the gun barrel had struck—sharp, insistent pulses that matched his heartbeat—but the pain felt distant, almost secondary. What Barker had said kept replaying in tight, looping fragments.

Kristof was innocent. Not just possibly innocent. Not just doubt-reasonable-enough-to-acquit.

Actually innocent.

Greyrock had ordered the hit. Professional. Clean. No trace.

Barker had loved her—really loved her—and still helped frame her husband to save his own skin.

Tomorrow, if Barker kept his word, he would walk into that courtroom and say it all under oath. No privilege. No dodging. Full exposure.

The case was over.

Kristof would walk free.

Avery exhaled, the breath ragged and visible in the cold air. For a moment the victory felt real—clean, bright, the kind of win that made every late night, every threat, every compromise worth it.

He could already picture Kristof's face when the not-guilty was read, the way his shoulders would drop, the way he'd look toward the public gallery as if seeing daylight for the first time in months.

Then the image shifted.

Rina crossing the street, Luca's hand in hers.

The telephoto compression.

The backpack label so clear it could have been taken from ten metres away.

The high came crashing down like cold water.

They weren't safe.

Not tonight.

Not tomorrow.

Not ever, if Greyrock decided the loose end named Avery Santos was still dangling.

Barker's warning echoed louder than the rain:

"They don't threaten. They act. Quietly. Cleanly. No loose ends."

Avery touched the gash on his forehead; his fingers came away wet with blood and rainwater. The pain sharpened everything. No more waiting for court to finish. No more assuming the bikies outside the flat were enough. Greyrock had already sent the photo. They had already told Barker to "deal with this problem." If Barker had changed his mind at the last second, someone else wouldn't hesitate.

He turned and started walking—fast, purposeful—back toward the car. The pier lights flickered behind him, weak and yellow.

By the time he reached the Commodore two blocks away, his shirt was soaked through, his head pounding in rhythm with his steps. The bikie in the driver's seat—big, bearded, plain black hoodie—looked up as Avery slid into the passenger seat.

"Everything alright, boss?"

"No," Avery said. "Change of plan. We're moving them now. Tonight. Not six am Not after court. Right fucking now."

The bikie didn't argue. He started the engine. "Where to?"

"First the flat. Then the hospice. Then somewhere Greyrock can't find them for at least a few days. Ollie's got a safe house—old fishing shack up near Brooklyn, Hawkesbury River. Off-grid, no address, cash only. Rina's mum can't travel far, but she can manage a short drive if we're careful."

The bikie nodded once, pulled out, tyres hissing on wet asphalt.

Avery pulled out his phone—Barker had switched it off but not taken it—and powered it back on. Three missed calls from Rina, two from Ollie.

He texted Rina first: *Coming home now. Pack essentials only—clothes, meds, Luca's bear. We're leaving tonight. I'll explain when I get there. Stay inside. Love you*

Then to Ollie: *Pier done. Barker's flipping—full testimony tomorrow. But Greyrock sent him to kill me. He didn't. Someone else will. Moving R + L + mum TONIGHT to Brooklyn shack. Need you to clear the route, sweep for tails. Bikies on point.*

Ollie's reply came in seconds:

On it. Two cars will meet you at the flat. Third will shadow to hospice. I'll be at the shack in 90. Stay sharp.

Avery leaned back against the headrest, eyes on the rain-streaked windscreen. The city blurred past—neon signs, wet tram tracks, late-night pedestrians under umbrellas. Ordinary life moving on while his own tilted toward something sharper, more dangerous.

He thought of Luca asleep in his pyjamas, Lego castle half-built on the living-room floor. Thought of Rina folding clothes into a bag with that quiet efficiency she used when she was scared but wouldn't show it.

Thought of Elle's kids—now Kristof's again, soon to be returned to a father who hadn't killed their mother but had still broken her heart.

Barker had asked him to watch over them.

Avery intended to keep that promise.

But first he had to keep his own family alive.

The Commodore turned into Rina's street. The two other bikie cars were already there—one parked across the road, one idling at the corner. Lights off. Engines low.

Avery stepped out into the rain, head still throbbing, blood mixing with water on his collar.

He climbed the stairs two at a time.

When Rina opened the door, duffel bag already at her feet, Luca asleep on her shoulder wrapped in a blanket, she didn't ask questions. She just looked at the bandage, the blood, the soaked clothes, and stepped aside so he could enter.

"Tell me on the way," she said quietly.

Avery took Luca from her arms—small, warm, trusting—and pressed his lips to the boy's hair.

"On the way," he agreed.

They left the flat without looking back.

Three cars pulled away in loose formation, headlights cutting through the rain toward the north.

Behind them, the city lights faded.

Ahead, the Hawkesbury waited—dark water, quiet bush, a temporary hiding place.

And somewhere in Sydney, Greyrock was already moving pieces of their own.

But for tonight, at least, Avery had bought them time.

Tomorrow he would finish what he started in Courtroom 11.

Tonight he would keep them breathing.

CHAPTER 23 CONFESSION

The courthouse clock read 9:47 am when Avery pushed through the heavy doors of Courtroom 11. His suit was the same one from yesterday—creased, rain-stained at the cuffs, the small bandage on his forehead now darkened at the edges with dried blood. He hadn't slept. The drive back from the Hawkesbury had taken most of the night: narrow winding roads, headlights cutting through fog, Rina beside him in the passenger seat holding Luca's sleeping form, Ollie trailing in the second car with the third bikie bringing up the rear. They'd arrived at the fishing shack just before dawn—timber walls, tin roof, no mobile signal, a wood stove already lit by Ollie's contact. Rina had kissed him once, fierce and wordless, before he turned the car around and drove straight back to the city.

He slipped into his seat at the defence table as quietly as possible. Kristof was already in the dock, looking across at him with quiet concern. Avery gave the smallest nod—*I'm here. We're good*—and opened his folder. His hands were steady, but his head still throbbed in dull waves.

"All rise."

Justice Bluegum entered, robes settling. The jury filed in, notebooks ready, faces drawn from weeks of sequestration.

Bluegum settled, adjusted his glasses. "Mr Santos, your final witness is available this morning?"

"Yes, Your Honour," Avery said, rising. "The defence calls Mr Daniel Lang, forensic gait analyst."

Lang entered: mid-fifties, bespectacled, precise step. He took the oath, credentials tendered—twenty years in biomechanics, expert in over fifty cases.

Avery approached the lectern. "Mr Lang, you analysed CCTV footage from the three burner-phone purchases and compared it to video of Detective Barker from court precinct cameras last week. What did you find?"

Lang gestured to the screen. Side-by-side videos played: hooded buyer on the left, Barker walking on the right. Slow-motion overlays highlighted left-leg favouring, shoulder roll, chin tuck.

"Gait is highly individual," Lang explained. "The buyer shows consistent left-side asymmetry from an old injury, matching Detective Barker's documented 2018 knee issue. Stride length 72 cm average, restrained left arm swing. Probabilistic match: 92%."

Turner cross-examined briefly: lighting, angles, clothing could distort. Lang conceded variables but stood firm: "The match holds under testing."

Bluegum directed the jury: "This evidence assists only in assessing reasonable possibility of alternative motive or explanation. It is not positive identification."

Avery thanked Lang. The witness stepped down.

Bluegum looked to the bar table. "Mr Santos, does the defence have any further evidence?"

"No, Your Honour," Avery said. "That concludes the defence case."

Bluegum nodded. "The defence case is closed."

A murmur moved through the gallery. Turner sat a little straighter, as if sensing the end.

But before Bluegum could begin his summing-up directions, Barker rose from the back row of the public gallery. Plain clothes, no tie, unshaven. He spoke clearly: "Your Honour, I request to be recalled. New information has come to light that I wish to place before the court."

The room froze.

Turner shot up. "Objection! The Crown case closed weeks ago. The defence has just closed. This is an attempt to re-open—"

Bluegum raised a hand. "Silence. Mr Barker, approach the bench with counsel."

A tense chambers conference followed—Turner arguing ambush, Avery arguing probative value and interests of justice. Bluegum listened, then ruled: "Given the proposed evidence directly relates to the alternative-motive theory already before the jury, and refusal could risk a miscarriage of justice, I will allow Detective Barker to be recalled. Limited to new matters only. The jury will assess his credibility accordingly."

They returned to the courtroom. Barker took the oath again.

Avery rose—no notes, no lectern. "Detective Barker, last night you contacted me and indicated you wished to provide further evidence. What do you wish to say?"

Barker looked straight at the jurors. "I was having an affair with Elle Stanis…"

The jury gasped in major shock.

"…It started six months before her death. Greyrock Developments hired me off-books to get close to her, use her position on the council approvals committee to flip the Marrickville project denial. They paid me. I did it. But it became real. I fell in love with her."

He paused, voice steady despite the hollow eyes.

"She found out. Confronted me. Said she was going to expose everything—to police, to the integrity unit. I begged her not to. She refused. Then she was dead.

Twenty-seven stab wounds. I didn't do it. Greyrock sent someone—professional, no trace. They told me to steer the investigation, frame her husband. I did. Because I was scared. Because if I didn't, they'd come for me next. And because part of me blamed Kristof for hurting her first."

Gasps rippled. Pens scratched furiously.

Turner seemed too caught up in the shock to object, this had changed everything. Turner was a professional though, so he rose and cross-examined hard—debts, lies under oath, motive to save himself. Barker answered each one: "Yes, I lied. Yes, I framed him. Yes, I'm finished. But this is the truth now."

Turner was disgusted, "if you are admitting to committing perjury and lying under oath – why should we believe anything, ANYTHING, you say now."

There was silence. Barker didn't answer, and just stared directly into Turner's eyes understanding his fate.

When Turner sat, Barker looked at Avery. "That's all I have."

Bluegum excused him. Barker walked out past the suits in the back row, who watched with flat, unreadable stares.

The courtroom held its breath.

For perhaps three seconds there was absolute silence—only the faint scratch of a reporter's pen and the soft creak of benches as people shifted.

Then Bluegum spoke, voice low but cutting through the room like a blade.

"Members of the jury, you will retire to the jury room immediately. Do not discuss anything you have just heard. You are not to deliberate or form any views on the evidence at this stage. The court will adjourn briefly."

The associate rose. "All rise."

The jury filed out, faces pale, eyes wide. Several glanced back at the now-empty witness box as if expecting Barker to reappear.

Once the door closed behind them, Bluegum turned to the bar table.

"Counsel, approach."

Avery and Turner walked forward. The associate remained at the bench; the court reporter paused her fingers.

Bluegum removed his glasses, rubbed the bridge of his nose once—a rare visible sign of strain—then replaced them.

"Mr Turner," he said quietly, "your position?"

Turner's voice was tight, controlled fury barely contained. "Your Honour, this is catastrophic. The witness has just confessed, on oath, to perverting the course of justice, misconduct in public office, and effectively accessory after the fact to murder. He has implicated a major corporate entity in a contract killing. None of this was foreshadowed. The Crown has closed its case. We have had no opportunity to test this evidence, obtain rebuttal material, or even consider whether Detective Barker should be charged in his own right. Continuing this trial would be fundamentally unfair to the Crown and would almost certainly result in a successful appeal by whichever party loses."

Bluegum looked at Avery.

"Mr Santos?"

Avery spoke carefully. "Your Honour, the defence submits that the interests of justice require the jury to hear this evidence in full. It goes directly to reasonable doubt. However, I acknowledge the procedural prejudice to the Crown, but we have an innocent man here rotting away for something he clearly did not do. My client has been in custody for many months on evidence that has now been substantially undermined by the lead investigator's own admission."

Bluegum was silent for a long moment. He looked toward the public gallery—empty now except for the lingering press and the two suits who had not moved. Then back to counsel. "This trial has been disrupted in a manner unprecedented in my experience on this bench," he said. "A senior police officer, the lead investigator, has confessed under oath to fabricating key aspects of the Crown case and to concealing the true perpetrator of the offence. That confession was not elicited by counsel; it was volunteered. The Crown has had no realistic opportunity to meet it. The jury has heard it in circumstances where no limiting direction could possibly cure the prejudice."

He paused again.

***

When the judge returned the jury, he then directed to them. He thanked them for their service but also apologised for the disruptions and concluded: "I am satisfied that continuing this trial would give rise to a substantial risk of a miscarriage of justice. The jury cannot realistically be expected to disregard what they have just heard, nor can the Crown fairly respond without time to investigate, obtain evidence, and consider whether to amend the indictment or discontinue the Prosecution." Bluegum straightened. "I therefore discharge the jury pursuant to the interests of justice and the Jury Act 1977. The jury is discharged without verdict."

A soft collective gasp moved through the remaining observers.

Bluegum continued, addressing both counsel, "Mr Turner, I expect the Director of Public Prosecutions will wish to review this matter urgently. Mr Santos, your client will remain in custody pending any further application. I will hear any urgent bail application tomorrow at 9:30 am if one is filed."

He rose.

The courtroom stood as Bluegum left the bench.

Kristof remained in the dock, stunned. The guards moved to escort him back to the cells, but he looked at Avery through the glass—eyes wide, questioning.

Avery stepped to the rail. "It's not over," he said quietly. "This buys us time. The Crown can't proceed on the old case now. They'll either drop it or start again. Either way, you're closer to walking than you were this morning. But I will file an urgent bail application tomorrow, and I believe you should be free tomorrow."

Kristof managed a small, shaky nod. "Thank you."

"Don't thank me," Avery said. "We aren't there yet."

***

Outside in the corridor, Ollie was waiting, arms folded, expression grim.

"Mistrial," Avery said before Ollie could ask.

Ollie exhaled. "Figured. LECC already has people moving on Barker. His flat's empty. Car's gone. No sign of him since he left the building."

Avery's stomach twisted. "Greyrock."

"Or he's running," Ollie said. "Either way, he's a dead man walking if they find him first."

Avery pulled out his phone and texted Rina:

Mistrial declared. Jury discharged. Kristof stays in custody for now, but case is collapsing. I'm coming up tonight. Stay where you are. Love you.

Her reply was instant:

I love you. We're safe. Luca's asleep. Hurry home. Be careful.

Avery pocketed the phone and looked at Ollie. "We need to get to the shack before dark. And we need to talk about what happens if the Crown drops the charges entirely."

Ollie nodded. "Greyrock won't care about a *nolle prosequi*. They'll still want loose ends tied off."

Avery straightened his stained jacket. "Then we don't give them any."

The rain was heavier now, drumming on the courthouse steps as they walked out.

The trial was over.

But Kristof wasn't free yet.

And the danger was only beginning.

CHAPTER 24 NOLLE PROSEQUI

THE DRIVE NORTH felt longer in the daylight, the rain easing to a patchy drizzle that smeared the windscreen under intermittent wipers. Avery gripped the wheel of the Commodore, Ollie silent in the passenger seat, the city receding in the rearview like a bad dream. Phillip Street, the marble corridors, Bluegum's bench—it all blurred into the grey horizon. But Kristof was still in Silverwater, Barker was in the wind, and the weight of what had happened in Courtroom 11 pressed down heavier than the mist.

Ollie broke the silence at the Harbour Bridge. "LECC called while you were inside. They want any evidence you have obtained regarding Barker, or they'll subpoena it from us. They've got a warrant for Barker's arrest—perverting justice, misconduct, the works.

Avery interjected assumptively, "Crown's likely reviewing the file tonight. They'll probably enter a *nolle prosequi* tomorrow. No point of a retrial on tainted evidence." Avery paused what he was saying and looked at Ollie, with a smirk. "I'm impressed, by the way. You've picked up a lot. Could make a have decent lawyer after all."

"Nah… I prefer the streets anyway."

Avery nodded once. "Alright, well I'll take care of the bail application and let's file it by tomorrow."

Ollie asked, "so what'll happen next?"

Avery answered, "Turner's not stupid—he knows the case is dead. Bluegum will likely end up granting bail, or Turner will drop the case against Kristof. Exceptional circumstances are a slam dunk now. If bail, then Kristof's no risk; he's got kids waiting, a job to go back to. Conditions will be light—report weekly, stay in NSW etc. Then inevitably the case will eventually get dropped in pursuit of Barker or whatever the real investigation turns up."

The Hawkesbury River came into view around dusk—wide, muddy brown under the fading light, mangroves hugging the banks. The shack was down a dirt track, hidden by eucalypts: single room, veranda facing the water, no neighbours for kilometres. Rina's car was parked out front, Luca's drawing taped to the window like a beacon.

Avery killed the engine. Ollie stayed in the car. "I'll take first watch. Go be with them."

Inside, the shack smelled of woodsmoke and instant coffee. Luca was at the small table, crayons scattered, building his Lego castle with fierce concentration. Rina stood by the stove, stirring something in a pot. She turned as the door creaked open, eyes lighting up despite the worry lines.

"You made it," she said softly.

Avery crossed the room in three steps, pulled her into his arms. She fit there perfectly—warm, solid, real. He buried his face in her hair, inhaling the faint scent of her shampoo mixed with river air.

"Missed you," he murmured.

She pulled back just enough to touch the bandage on his forehead. "How's your head?"

"It's okay… Long day. But it's over. Mistrial. Kristof's free tomorrow—bail hearing at 9:30. Crown's likely dropping the case."

Her eyes widened. "Free? As in…"

"As in acquitted, effectively. No retrial. The evidence is poisoned. Not confirmed yet, but I believe it'll happen tomorrow."

Luca looked up from his Lego. "Avery! Look—the dragon's trapped now! And mum said we're on holiday!"

Avery knelt beside him, admiring the wobbly towers. "Best castle I've seen. Dragon-proof for sure."

Luca beamed, then yawned. Rina glanced at the clock. "Bedtime soon, little man. Finish your masterpiece tomorrow."

Later, with Luca asleep on the fold-out couch, Avery and Rina sat on the veranda steps. The river lapped quietly below; stars punched through the clouds. She leaned against his shoulder.

"We're safe here?" she asked.

"For now. Ollie's outside. Bikies rotating watches. Barker's gone dark—LECC can't find him. But the confession's on record. Crown's shifting focus. Greyrock's exposed, even if they're still untouchable for the moment."

She traced his hand with her fingers. "And us? When do we go home?"

"Soon. After the bail hearing. I'll wrap things with Kristof, then we disappear for a bit—real holiday, no shadows. But truthfully, Barker did me a favour today. I hope Greyrock are more concerned about him than us. No matter what though, I'll take care of us."

She smiled—small, real. "I love you. You know that?"

He kissed her then—slow, deep, the kind that said everything words couldn't. "I love you more. We're through the worst."

They sat like that until the chill drove them inside, falling asleep tangled together on the narrow bed, Luca's soft breathing the only sound.

***

Morning came too soon. Avery drove back alone at dawn, Ollie staying behind to watch the shack. The bail hearing was short—Bluegum presiding again, Turner conceding the Crown would not oppose. "In light of recent developments, the Director has instructed a *nolle prosequi* be entered. We will not proceed to retrial."

Bluegum stated almost too quickly, "in light of the Crown's position, the proceedings against you, Kristof Stanis, are stayed. The indictment is quashed. You are formally discharged and free to go."

And just like that. The case was done. Kristof was a free man.

The reporters gathered outside the Court steps. Avery hoped this would happen so he could send a message.

After the reporters asked a barrage of questions asking how it felt for himself, and his client, and Avery providing his typical "justice is served" responses. One reporter finally asked the question he was waiting for, "Mr Santos, in light of everything said in Court about Greyrock, what next steps will you take?"

"Nothing. I was only here to defend my client, who was innocent of the charges laid against him. In terms of investigations and digging – that's not my job. My job is done."

He hoped it would send a message of truce to Greyrock, that he was going to be steering clear of them – hopeful that they would steer clear of him.

Avery shook his hand outside. "You're done. Go home to your kids."

Kristof's eyes were wet. "I owe you everything."

Avery said. "Just live clean, and take care of your kids."

As Kristof drove away, Avery's phone stayed silent. No messages. No warnings. Just the quiet aftermath.

Back at the shack that evening, Rina and Luca were waiting.

CHAPTER 25 SAFE FOR NOW

AFTER A WEEK away and no noise, they packed up, drove home under clear skies. Life resumed—Luca to school, Rina to work, Avery to chambers.

Two weeks later, a small envelope arrived at the flat. No sender. Inside: a single photo of Elle Stanis crossing the road with her kids – the same photo from Barker's phone that night on the pier. On the back, handwritten in unfamiliar script: *They're safe. For now. -B*

Avery stared at it for a long time. Then he burned it in the sink that night, watching the edges curl black.

Barker had vanished entirely—LECC's warrant still active, no trace.

Greyrock issued a bland press release about "cooperating with authorities" and "internal reviews." Denying any involvements in the death of Elle. No arrests. No charges.

Kristof returned to his kids, to his life, quiet and grateful.

And Avery knew: the guilt's shadow wasn't gone.

It was just waiting—patient, silent, somewhere out of sight. With Greyrock's resources, he knew it wasn't over, knew that with everything going on they were laying low for now. Avery knew, but in this moment, the flat was warm, Luca's laughter filled the rooms, and Rina's hand found his in the dark.

They breathed.

They lived.

And that, for the moment, was enough.

CHAPTER 26 GUILT'S SHADOW

THREE MONTHS HAD passed since the case and the workflow was steady as normal. It was the first time since the trials end that he'd thought of Kristof or Barker. He had been too consumed with ensuring Greyrock's presence had vacated from his life, that he hadn't had a chance to rest. Sitting in his new home office, still with some unpacked boxes, Rina and Avery had decided on moving in together not long after the trial had ended. Now, he finally felt like he could slow down, his mind had was able to relax.

He snapped his attention back to his desk, where the folders and documents had been piling up. To anyone else observing it would have been an indiscernible scatter of paperwork, but to Avery, he knew that his upcoming cases were in the folders on the left side of his desk, the yellow legal pads throughout the centre were his priority cases, and to his right side were miscellaneous but important documents. These included anything from office bills and expenses to resumes of applicants who'd applied to work for his firm. He picked the first one up, and scanned through the cover letter and resume quickly.

Rina, sitting with him, asked, "so, are you finally going to hire some associates?"

"I'm not sure yet. The help would be nice, but inevitably that's going to require more time spent training and explaining."

Just as he put the application down, he noticed in the corner of miscellaneous documents, the envelope he had received months back. He knew it was empty. He'd burned the photo he received from Barker. He thought about Barker, Kristof, Elle, the children, for one final time. He put the application down, grabbed the empty envelope and threw it in the rubbish bin. It was as if this act was his final closure of the case and all the events that had followed—he could finally lay it to rest, he thought.

Rina wrapped her arms around his waist and tucked herself in close to his chest before looking up to kiss him as they embraced.

Avery hugged back and continued, "you know there's something I was thinking about during that whole case."

"What's that baby?"

"Well, I could sense the guilt hanging over all these people involved. Following them like a cloud –"

"-or a shadow."

"Exactly. I still wondered why Barker turned all of a sudden, you see he really despised me and worked hard to push me off the scent and trail. But when we got there in the end, I thought it was the pressure that changed his tune… but it was Elle… it was the guilt. That shadow, like you call it, that was following him around, guilt's shadow. That eventually pushed him into the light, and for some it consumes them, others it makes them act. For Barker, it made him act, to do the right thing in the end."

"and who else?"

"Huh?"

"You said you could sense the guilt hanging over 'all these people' – who else?"

"Oh right. Well, Kristof too actually. Even though I believed he didn't kill his wife, I still sensed something off about him. He may have been innocent of something, but he was guilty of something else. And something Barker told me that night on the pier didn't actually sink in right away. Everyone knew of Elle's affair, but no one knew of Kristof's affair first. I feel like a part of him still felt guilty about that and was partly the reason why he helped drive her away into Barker's arms. Maybe that's what he was still feeling guilty about."

"I don't think you can say that if he didn't have an affair, then she would still be alive."

"No no, not at all… I am just saying… I guess, that guilt can cast a long shadow."

CHAPTER 27 12:03AM

KRISTOF RETURNED HOME after having drinks with the guys from work. It was 11:48pm on the dashboard clock of his car.

He felt drained from the day, but this feeling was something he had been carrying for weeks. Ever since she told him about the affair.

He knew he would bracing for a fight. They had agreed to a date night, and sent the kids to their grandparent's house for the evening. His last-minute message at the end of the day, wasn't just a text saying he would be late from work, instead it was a blow in an attempt to show how mad he was at her still.

He sat there and stared, unsure of whether to go inside or not. Maybe he would sleep in his car again, maybe not.

He felt the rush of emotions, from anger to jealousy to betrayal, to sympathy and understanding.

The conversations from the weeks prior were playing in his head:

"Kristof, please… I love you. I love you and our kids. I told you this because I want to rebuild with you." He thought of those words from weeks beforehand when she confessed.

"How fucking dare you? You love me? And you fuck someone else! That's bullshit."

"No Kristof, I know… I felt the exact same way last year remember – when I caught you."

"Oh here we go again! I told you I'd ended it!"

"But I caught you Kristof! Who knows what would have happened if I never caught you – and I still gave you a chance, because you begged me to! And this time, you didn't catch me. I went out by myself and I came back – I wanted to hurt you because you had hurt me. And I did, but I hurt us both. So, instead of trying to play some bullshit mind games and play tit for tat – I am coming clean to you because I truly want to make this work. I have betrayed us… but I want this relationship to work. Please."

He kept arguing with her in the middle of his mind, reeling and feeling all of it.

Please please please – he thought to himself, whilst staring at the clock. It read 12:03am now on the dashboard.

He decided he would give it a chance. He would continue to fight for her, the same way she fought for him when he messed up.

He walked into the house and the sight was something he was not expecting and completely unprepared for…

There in the middle of their garage, lay Elle, covered with stab wounds through her darkly soaked shirt, in a pool of blood. He rushed over immediately seeking her aid and touch of her body! Ellle – he cried. What's happened! Oh god oh god! I should have come home.

He saw the knife still in her, he grabbed it, but he knew better than to pull it out.

She was still conscious with the lightest breath and tiniest sign of life. She said, "I'm sorry Kristof. I love you."

"Hold on baby. I am calling the ambulance, just stay with me!"

He grabbed his phone from his pocket, and immediately dialled 000. By the time he glanced back down, her body suddenly looked lifeless.

He leaned over, shouting her name to try and wake her. It was too late. She was gone.

Author's Note

This is a work of fiction. Names, characters, businesses, places, events, and incidents are either the products of the author's imagination or used in a fictitious manner. Any resemblance to actual persons, living or dead, or actual events is purely coincidental. While the courtroom procedures, police investigations, and legal frameworks in Guilt's Shadow draw from real practices in the Supreme Court of New South Wales and the broader Australian criminal justice system, I have taken liberties for dramatic pacing and storytelling—such as condensing timelines, simplifying certain evidentiary rules, and fictionalising elements of development approvals and corruption inquiries. For example, the Australian court system does not use gavels, so some of the dramatization is purely for storytelling effect. The story is not based on any specific real case, person, or scandal.

The idea for this novel grew from my fascination with how guilt—personal, moral, and institutional—can cast a long shadow over lives, even when justice appears to prevail. In a system designed to seek truth, the cracks where doubt, fear, and compromise seep in are often the most human parts. I wanted to explore that through characters who carry their burdens quietly, much like the everyday people who pass through Sydney's courts every day. Writing this book was a labour of love, born from late nights and endless revisions. Thank you for reading it. If the story lingered with you—even just a little—then I've done what I set out to do.

If you would like more works from us; the writer and the team, please feel free to email at maquinoarturo@gmail.com.